She opened the drawer and pulled a condom...

"Oh, my God, Portia, this is like a fantasy come true," Rourke groaned, "but I'm not sure I'm up to it. Wait. What the hell am I saying? The sexiest woman in the universe is standing next to my bed, unwrapping a condom. Hell, yes, I'm up to it. You'll have to do most of the work, but still..."

It took Portia's hormonally oversaturated brain about a nanosecond to imagine herself pulling off her clothes and going for a ride.

She picked up an ice cube. "I'm making you an ice pack. For your back."

"Oh." Rourke lay there for a second, his eyes closed. It was suddenly incredibly hot in his room. Portia proceeded to pack ice into the penis-shaped rubber, struggling to hold it still. Damn, why had she grabbed a lubricated one?

"Okay, I've just forfeited all my pride today, so I'll just confess that I can't watch you do that. Or let's just say that I shouldn't," he admitted.

Portia felt a surge of sexual power. She stood there teasing him with her deliberate stroking movements. The sexual energy between them made her feel almost drunk.

"You're a wicked woman, Portia Tomlinson." Rourke choked out the words. "But I wouldn't have you any other way...."

Note from the editor...

An Evening To Remember... Those words evoke all kinds of emotions and memories. How do you plan a romantic evening with your guy that will help you get in touch with each other on every level?

Start with a great dinner that you cook together. Be sure to light several candles and put fresh flowers on the table. Enjoy a few glasses of wine and pick out your favorite music to set the mood. After dinner take the time to really talk to each other. Hold hands and snuggle on the sofa in front of the fireplace. And maybe take a few minutes to read aloud selected sexy scenes from your favorite Harlequin Temptation novel. After that, anything can happen....

That's just one way to have an evening to remember. There are so many more. Write and tell us how you keep the spark in your relationship. And don't forget to check out our Web site at www.eHarlequin.com.

Sincerely,

Birgit Davis-Todd
Executive Editor

JENNIFER LaBRECQUE
REALLY HOT!

HARLEQUIN®

TORONTO • NEW YORK • LONDON
AMSTERDAM • PARIS • SYDNEY • HAMBURG
STOCKHOLM • ATHENS • TOKYO • MILAN • MADRID
PRAGUE • WARSAW • BUDAPEST • AUCKLAND

ISBN 0-373-69212-9

REALLY HOT!

www.eHarlequin.com

Printed in U.S.A.

Dear Reader,

A look across a crowded room...the flight of butterflies in your tummy...the slow tingle of awareness down your spine...the sizzle of the briefest touch. This is chemistry, the magic elixir of romance, the inexplicable, undeniable blossom of attraction between two people.

That's what finally happens to Rourke O'Malley. Rourke made his first appearance in "The Last Virgin," the final story in the anthology *Getting Real*. What a guy! The proverbial Mr. Tall, Dark and Handsome, and a nice guy to boot, Rourke had hero written all over him. Unfortunately, the heroine of the story, Andrea Scarpini had other ideas....

But a potential hero is a terrible thing to waste. How could I just let this awesome, sexy guy walk away? There was only one thing to do...find him some chemistry. And what better way than to give this hottie his own reality TV show, complete with a bevy of beauties to choose from? Only, the woman he wants is "don't go there" associate producer and single mom Portia Tomlinson.

I hope you enjoy reading Portia and Rourke's story as much as I loved writing it. The only thing I like better than writing is hearing from readers. You can look me up at www.jenniferlabrecque.com or drop me a note by snail mail at P.O. Box 298, Hiram, GA 30141.

Happy reading...

Jennifer LaBrecque

Books by Jennifer LaBrecque

HARLEQUIN TEMPTATION
886—BARELY MISTAKEN
904—BARELY DECENT
952—BARELY BEHAVING
992—BETTER THAN CHOCOLATE

HARLEQUIN DUETS
28—ANDREW IN EXCESS
52—KIDS+COPS=CHAOS
64—JINGLE BELL BRIDE?

To Leslie Kelly, Julie Elizabeth Leto
and Vicki Lewis Thompson, talented writers
and extraordinary people, and the chemistry behind
GETTING REAL.

1

"Rourke O'Malley is an orgasm waiting to happen," Portia Tomlinson read aloud. She rolled her eyes and scrolled down the screen, following the postings on the fan site for *The Last Virgin*, the latest reality show she'd worked on as associate producer. "Give me a break. Some women don't have good sense."

Rourke had been the favored contestant, but the show's bachelorette hadn't picked him. He had, however, captured the hearts of female viewers around the world and they were in a veritable lust frenzy. Amazing. She swung around in her office chair.

"You mean you don't think he's an orgasm waiting to happen?" Sadie Franken, an administrative assistant, asked.

More than once, Rourke O'Malley had intruded on Portia's dreams, but she wasn't about to make that public knowledge. And she wasn't happy about it, either. Portia shrugged. "He's okay. Great face, great body, but that's nothing new in Hollywood. Of course, this—" she gestured over her shoulder toward the computer screen "—should mean great ratings for our new show." This time around, they'd signed Rourke on as their star bachelor and lined up twelve wealthy single women for him to choose from. She'd read an article citing that the latest trend among the twenty-something idle rich was to push their parents' buttons by putting themselves in a controversial spotlight. They had twelve young women who were living proof. Portia, however, was the lucky duck saddled with baby-sitting Rourke, the star, through production. She eyed the petite redhead. "Obviously you've joined the legion of women ready to drop at his feet."

Sadie raised her hand. "Guilty as charged. I've enjoyed several orgasms with him lately. I just crank my vibrator, close my eyes and Rourke O'Malley and I have a grand time."

Brash and uninhibited, Sadie usually left Portia laughing. "*That* was so much more information than I *ever* wanted to know. Please feel free *not* to share in the future."

Sadie arched a brow. "Can you honestly tell me you've never fantasized about him after working with him and seeing him day after day?" Portia opened her mouth but Sadie cut her off before she could utter the denial. "You've never thought about kissing that fabulous mouth? Never imagined that hot bod naked and sweaty and getting down? Never imagined him touching you, you touching him?"

Enough. "No, no and no. I haven't." But now thanks to Sadie, she had. A warm flush spread inside her and she mercilessly exorcized the erotic imagery.

"Well maybe you should—"

"Not." Portia cut her off and finished the sentence. "I should not."

"A little fantasy never hurt anyone."

"I don't have time for fantasy." And if she craved the time, reality lurked right around the corner. The stark contrast between the two proved too painful. Portia lived in the here and now.

She'd found out nine years ago where fantasy got you—single, pregnant and shattered. The ensuing reality had been waiting tables, changing diapers, several long years of night school and working her butt off to get ahead and make a better life for her and Danny.

Sadie shook her head. "A woman without time for fantasy. That's just not right."

Portia grinned. "Sorry, toots."

"When's the last time you had a date?"

She shrugged and lied. "Not that long ago."

"Ha. Name the day, place and man."

Sadie was fun and they laughed together, but she'd just crossed into *nunya* territory, as in none of your business. Portia'd had one date in the last nine, almost ten, years. She had neither the time nor the inclination. Guys thought single moms were easy marks, desperate for sex. Thanks, but no thanks. The only thing she was desperate for was more hours in the day and a good pedicure.

Portia smiled to herself. Poor Sadie'd really be wrecked if she knew Portia hadn't had sex since the last time she'd slept with Mark, Danny's dad—wait, Mark hadn't been a dad at all, make that sperm donor—just before she found out she was pregnant. Sweet-talking, pretty-boy Mark, who'd promised to love her forever, had dumped her before the word *pregnant* was out of her mouth. And he'd turned out to be one rung lower than a deadbeat dad. The last she'd heard, he was a crackhead shacked up in East L.A.

"You're not going to answer me are you?" Sadie asked.

"Nope." Portia smiled to take the sting out of it.

"Well, okay. Don't date, don't fantasize. I'll handle all of that for both of us." Sadie nodded toward the computer screen crammed with fan postings. "Me and the other women without good sense."

"Good deal. You can drool enough for both of us."

"What a wasted opportunity. It's not fair you get to spend a couple of weeks shooting this new show with him. Fourteen days in a romantic setting with those blue eyes, that black hair, those chiseled features, that body…I've got chills just thinking about it."

"I know." Portia heaved a dramatic sigh, fluttered her lashes, and cooed in a falsetto voice. "Just me, him, the moonlight, the hot tub…" Portia lost the simpering tone and added dryly, "…a dozen poor little rich girls and a production crew. Cozy, intimate."

"Go ahead, make fun. I'd be content just to breathe the same air he does."

"You need to breathe a little more air *now* instead of waiting on O'Malley. Obviously your brain isn't getting enough oxygen." Portia glanced out the window. "Are we on red alert today?"

Actually, she thought the Santa Ana winds had blown through and temporarily cleared the wretched smog that smothered the city so badly that they issued breathing codes.

"Very funny."

"I was just reminding you that even if I were re-motely interested in Boy Toy O'Malley, and I think we've established that I'm not, he's there to pick from a bevy of wealthy beauties and I'm a drone, there to produce a show that'll pull in ratings."

"Drone? That has such an ugly sound to it."

"Ah, but apropos." And nothing was going to stop her. This was her proving ground. One last two-weeker away on location. If she did well, she'd been promised a studio position. No more long stretches of time away on location, when Danny had to stay with her parents and her sister. He loved them and they loved him, but the poor kid only had one parent as it was. He deserved to have her around a little more. Yeah, she'd still work brutal hours, but she *would* be home every night and he'd wake up to her there every morning. She had high stakes riding on this assignment.

"I WANT to have your baby!"

Rourke ducked into the elevator and watched in horror as the woman chasing him brandished a pair of purple thong panties and almost lost a few fingers in the closing door. "I love you," she yelled, dropping the panties and yanking her hand out at the last minute. "Call me."

He slumped against the wall, relieved the stranger, nutso or not, wasn't an amputee because of him. "The whole world's gone insane."

"Nah, man. Just the female portion. And, yeah, they're all crazy about you," his baby brother Nick said.

"I'm pretty sure I'm crazy agreeing to do this show and all of…this." He gestured at the undies on the floor. No way. A piece of paper with a phone number was pinned in the crotch. Totally looney.

"You're a good brother. You know I appreciate what you're doing for me." Despite his words, Rourke wasn't sure whether Nick realized exactly how close he'd come to jail time. Embezzlement was a constant and serious temptation when you handled large quantities of money on a daily basis, and it had been a temptation his baby brother hadn't resisted. If Nick returned the money, his employer had agreed not to press charges, preferring his money back to bad publicity. "Although choosing from twelve beautiful women with more money than God…I don't know how much of a hardship that'll be, bro."

Nick really was clueless. "When people have that much money, they think they *are* God," Rourke said. He knew. He worked with them on a daily basis.

"Okay, sorry I sounded like an ingrate. Ya know, I can't thank you enough for helping me come up with the money." The elevator door opened.

Rourke checked out the hallway for any other lingerie-wielding women. Coast was clear. He stepped over the purple thong. With a shrug, Nick scooped the panties up and shoved them in his pocket. "And you were right about not telling Ma and Da, it would've killed them."

Paul and Moira O'Malley had worked hard all their lives for a neat little house and yard in Quincey and an almost-comfortable retirement. They took pride in hard work, their home and their kids. If they knew how off-track Nicky had gotten…the shame of embezzlement and prison would indeed damn near kill them. Not to mention they wouldn't hesitate to impoverish themselves trying to help him out of his jam. And Rourke wouldn't see that happen, or he'd die trying.

As an investment banker, he made decent money. *Investment* being the key word—most of his money was tied up. Ready cash simply wasn't that ready. Nick had pointed out that reality-TV winners could bring in big bucks. It had seemed like a longshot, but more palatable than a loan shark.

It was too bad Nick couldn't have been the one on the show. Nick had good looks and the charm to go with it. Having all those women acting crazy about Rourke was just testimony to the power of suggestion and slick PR hype. In the last twelve years, his braces had come off, he'd filled out a hell of a lot and traded in pop-bottle glasses for contact lenses, but Rourke knew he was a geek beneath it all. And he still found mixing and mingling difficult. He could talk financial investments all day, but outside of that, he was pretty much at a loss. He'd heard himself referred to as the strong, silent type, which made him feel even more like a fraud because he knew he was the quiet, I-don't-know-what-to-say geeky type. The truth of the matter was, women sort of scared the hell out of him.

But here he was, having blown the first opportunity to cash in on reality TV, moving on to round two, a sure thing to bring in the cash and keep Nick out of prison.

He unlocked his apartment door and Nick followed him in. He'd lived here two years and still loved the view from his place, the mix of modern skyscrapers, pre-Revolutionary redbrick buildings and Boston's legendary harbor.

"Thanks for looking after my place while I'm gone. Watson'll be much happier at home this time." Hearing his name, the miniature schnauzer jumped down from the recliner he shared with Rourke and trotted over to him. Rourke bent down to scratch him behind the ears. "We'll go for a walk in a minute." He straightened and Watson walked over to sit patiently at the door. "You know Mom and Dad aren't really dog people."

Watson had stayed with his parents during the taping of *The Last Virgin*. Not only had poor Watson lost the comfort of his recliner, he'd been relegated to the yard. This time around, Nick was staying at Rourke's place and dogsitting.

"It's cool. Wats and I are buds, but I hate scooping up the crap when he goes for a walk." Nick shuddered, wearing a look of disgust.

Rourke laughed with something close to incredulity. Nick could be so damned self-absorbed it amazed Rourke. "Probably not nearly as much as you'd hate being some tattooed felon's prison bitch. Keep that in mind while you're cleaning up after Watson. It'll put all the crap in your life in perspective."

Nick winced. "Where's a poop-scoop bag? Bring it on."

Rourke grabbed Watson's leash and passed the requested bag to Nick. Case in point, Rourke thought as he laughed with genuine amusement, it was impossible to stay angry with Nick.

"I'd love to trade places with you," Rourke said as they headed back out the door, Watson leading the way. He shuddered thinking about the next couple of weeks. It hadn't been so bad on the last show, a bunch of guys and one woman. And he and Andrea, the bachelorette now known around the world as The Virgin, had actually become friends. If they'd been on the set a bit longer he thought he might've become friends with the Goth-clad lead camera woman, Jacey, as well. Jacey was a bit of an odd fit and he'd instinctively known she wouldn't mind if he was a geek. But this time, it was only him and a legion of spoiled, high-maintenance women. And Portia Tomlinson.

He'd had mixed emotions when the studio listed her as associate producer. Portia fascinated him. Despite her friendly, easy demeanor, she had a way of looking at him with a trace of disdain, as if she'd judged him and found him lacking in some way. Perhaps if she got to know him better….

He'd thought about asking her out after the last show but they'd immediately offered him this upcoming show. And then there was the matter of him living in Boston and her living in LA. And those were both nice excuses. The ugly truth was he'd figured she'd turn him down so fast it'd leave his head spinning. "Trust me, I'd rather clean up after Watson than be hounded by those pampered princesses."

They got on the elevator.

Nick, who ran through women the way a slots addict in Vegas runs through a bag of coins, shook his head. "You are seriously warped, Rourke. Like, maybe you need some therapy. I can't say I understand it, but I appreciate your sacrifice." Nick punched him on the shoulder. "Who knows? A dozen hot women, you might find your own true love."

Maybe he did need therapy. Twelve women and he was half smitten already with a woman who wasn't available. "Yeah."

"I don't want to step on your toes or anything, but I could give you some pointers. You know, I do okay with women," Nick said. *That* was an understatement.

Rourke wasn't exactly hitting any home runs on his own. Portia had treated him as if he were a piece of furniture, a prop, on the last show. And he didn't want to humiliate himself by bombing with the twelve women. Best possible scenario would be to drag Nick along, a modern version of Cyrano de Bergerac, but that was impossible. He supposed the next best thing would be pointers. "I think I can use all the help I can get."

The door opened and Rourke was relieved to find the lobby empty. Nick shoved the poop bag into his pocket and grinned, "Welcome to Women 101."

PORTIA SCHLEPPED her suitcase along the service hallway of the mansion set high in the hills overlooking Hollywood. She grinned to herself. One of the first of many differences between a drone and a princess. Drones carried their own baggage.

"Can I help you with that?" The low, rich baritone slid across her skin, leaving a trail of gooseflesh in its wake. That voice belonged to the man who had haunted her dreams and left her discontented and frustrated the last couple of nights. O'Malley.

She pasted on a smile and glanced over her shoulder without breaking stride. "Thanks, but I've got it."

Oh. Those startling blue eyes were right over her shoulder. He was closer than she'd thought.

"It's no trouble," he said.

She bit back the comment, *save it for the princesses, pretty boy, they're gonna run you ragged,* reminding herself O'Malley was her star and it was her job to keep him happy. If he wanted to schlep for her then who was she to stand in his way? She stopped. "Well, thank you then, if it's no trouble."

She relinquished her suitcase, his fingers brushing hers in the exchange. A slight tremor ran through her and the hallway suddenly seemed narrow and confining. His broad shoulders took up an inordinate amount of space and his subtle scent surrounded her.

Since the filming and subsequent airing of their previous show, *The Last Virgin*, the seemingly impossible had happened. Rourke O'Malley looked even better than he had before. Portia's gaze stopped on the top two buttons of his golf shirt, which were unbuttoned, revealing a smattering of dark hair and tanned skin. She glanced up. For a second his eyes held hers and something passed between them that Portia didn't want to acknowledge. Drawing a deep breath, she turned away from him. "It's this way."

"I'm following you," he said.

They started back down the hall and Portia scrambled to dispel the awareness that lingered between them, to get things back on the friendly, light footing she maintained with all her co-workers. He was just another cast member and the good-looking guys never tired of hearing how...well, how good they looked. "You're looking great. Obviously the adoration of thousands agrees with you." She offered a smile.

O'Malley shook his head and looked embarrassed. Not the faux embarrassment so many handsome men adopted, but genuinely loosen-his-collar embarrassed. "The whole thing is crazy." They turned a corner. "A woman chased me onto an elevator this week to give me her underwear...with her name and number pinned in the crotch."

It was both funny and slightly erotic. Portia couldn't choke back her laughter. O'Malley shot her a censoring look. "I hope she wasn't wearing them at the time and I hope they were nice."

He shook his head again, a glimmer of a smile in his startlingly blue eyes. "She had them in her hand. Purple thong. She offered to have my baby."

He wasn't boasting. It was more as if he were still reeling from the weirdness of it. It just confirmed Portia's earlier assertion that some women had lost it over this guy.

"Well, the burning question is, did you call her?" Portia couldn't resist teasing him.

"No. I didn't call her," he said, indignantly. Then he looked rather sheepish. "But you already knew that, didn't you?"

"Yeah, I did, but I'm glad you confirmed it for me," she said, stopping at the room door marked on the site map as hers. Go figure, the mansion was so huge, they'd armed the production crew with maps. And all of a sudden, she realized she'd been as relaxed, but still aware of O'Malley as a man instead of just a cast member, as she'd ever been. Which effectively dispelled any lingering camaraderie.

"Well, this is it." She opened the door and turned for her suitcase, "I've got it. Thanks so much."

O'Malley acted as if he hadn't heard her and brought her luggage into the room. He glanced around at the single dresser and unframed mirror, the ladderback chair, uncarpeted concrete floor, his gaze finally settling on the narrow bed that was little more than a cot. "This is…minimalist."

It was positively Spartan.

"You and the pri—" she caught herself in the nick of time, she had to stop thinking of the contestants as princesses "—contestants are housed in guest rooms. The crew, except for Lauchmann and Daniels—" the producer and director "—well, the rest of us get the slave quarters."

Like a change in the wind, the atmosphere between them shifted. O'Malley flicked his eyes over her and heat seared her. "It's hard to imagine you as anyone's slave," the husky note in his voice fired her imagination.

"I don't take orders well. Do you?"

"It depends on what's being asked of me," he said. His glance slid over her. "And who's doing the asking. Speaking of… How does our relationship work?"

"Our relationship?"

"During the filming."

Of course. "Well, I need you to cooperate. If I ask you to be somewhere or do something, if you could accommodate that? On the other hand, it's my job to make sure you're satisfied—" that didn't sound right "—that your needs are met—" oy, that sounded even worse, next he'd think she'd be offering her underwear with a phone number "—if you need anything, please let me know."

"Anything?" He quirked a dark eyebrow and her heart knocked hard against her ribs.

"Within reason." She squashed his suggestive note.

"I'll try to keep my requests…reasonable."

"I appreciate that. And I don't think you'll find me too demanding." What was wrong with her? Why did *demanding* seem fraught with sexual innuendo?

"I'm more than willing to accommodate any of your demands. Just let me know." Rourke hefted her suitcase to the bed which didn't give an inch. "This bed is like a brick. Do you like it hard?"

It'd been so long she couldn't remember...and that was *so* not what he meant. He'd awakened some sexual energy she'd thought was long gone. But obviously she wasn't immune to drop-dead gorgeous O'Malley standing by her bed asking her if she liked it hard. The thought alone made her shiver inside. "I'm sure it will be fine."

"This hardly seems fair compared to our rooms."

"Oh, come on. Could you imagine Tara Mitchells in here?" Tara's father was an oil mogul. Or was he the real estate mogul? All the fathers were moguls, it merely varied by industry. "Or maybe one of the gaffers bunking down next to her?"

"Okay. You've got a point."

"Plus, we've got security in place that rivals Fort Knox. If some looney or terrorist group decided they wanted some ready cash, they could pick up twelve hostages, whose families' combined wealth is more than that of some small nations, in one fell swoop."

Rourke nodded. "I'd thought about that too. The studio's taking some pretty big chances on *Pick a Date with the Rich and Beautiful*."

Portia's surprise must've shown through.

"What?" Rourke asked.

"You're one of them."

Rourke laughed. "Not by a long shot. I'm not rich. I do okay, but I'll never be in the same league as any of their wealth—"

"Unless you marry one of them."

"Nobody said a word about marriage and I read the fine print on my contract. But even if I went there, it's still not my wealth is it? And as for being beautiful, the panties and all of that, it's just media hype. I know what I look like."

"And so do the women of the world. You're an incredibly handsome man, O'Malley, but then I have a hard time believing you don't already know that." She said it dispassionately, impersonally, as if she were observing the weather. In Hollywood, good looks were a commodity.

He shook his head. "My brother got the looks in the family."

There was another O'Malley that looked *better* than him? "God help the women of the world." And she mentally made a note to pass the info along to PR.

Her cell phone rang and her mother's number flashed on caller ID. "Excuse me. I need to take this call." She turned her back to him, dismissing him and the sexual energy he exuded. She flipped the phone open. "Hello."

"Hi, Mom," Danny said.

"Hey, you." She walked over to the small window that overlooked the back kitchen entrance.

"Are you busy?" He'd learned always to ask if

she was tied up on the job. Every time she left home for a location, he called the first day or so. Poor guy. He was amazingly flexible and resilient, but it was an adjustment for him every time she traveled. It'd be nice to move into the studio job.

"No, I'm not too busy. What are you doing?" A white-jacketed cook stepped out of the kitchen door and lit up a cigarette.

"Nothing. I just wanted to make sure you got there okay."

"I did. This house is cool. You'd love it."

They talked for a minute about his day and she assured him she missed him before she ended the call.

"Love you, Danny. I'll call you tonight."

She snapped the phone shut and turned around, surprised to find O'Malley still by her bed.

"Oh, I thought you'd left," she said.

"I just had one more question for you." He shifted his weight to his other foot and nodded toward her phone. "Boyfriend?"

Portia shook her head. "The love of my life." Her private life was her own business and let him make of that what he would. And maybe that would block this energy, this awareness, that seemed to flow between them.

"So you don't need to go on a TV show to find someone special?"

They couldn't pay her enough. "No. I have someone special waiting at home." This was much better. Now if she could just get him out of her room before she found herself mired in more inappropriate thoughts. "Thanks for bringing my suit-case. I'll see you at the briefing."

She all but pushed him out into the hall and closed the door behind him. She blew out a deep breath and realized O'Malley'd never asked the question he'd waited around to ask. Too bad, so sad. She'd needed him out of her room. He had a way of invading her space, getting under her skin, unnerving her.

She opened her suitcase on the bed. O'Malley's scent lingered—or was it all in her head? *Do you like it hard?* She felt flushed. God help her, but her nipples hardened just thinking about the lazy challenge in his deep-blue eyes. Her hands shook slightly as she unpacked her underwear.

She had a feeling this was going to be a very long two weeks.

ROURKE WANDERED BACK through the mansion, fasci-nated by the architectural details in the house and disquieted by his encounter with Portia Tomlinson. She was pleasant, complimentary even, but he still had the feeling she disliked him. No. That wasn't exactly true. It was something between dislike and dismissal. She'd told him how handsome he was and even with her dispassionate tone, it'd meant more than all the crazy rantings Nick had shown him on a Web site. Pathetic really. When she'd laughed and teased him over the purple panties, she'd been different—more accessible, not so dis-tant—which only accentuated the other.

And the change in her when she'd taken that

phone call—there'd been a softness about her. What kind of man brought that look to her face? She'd deemed the caller, Danny, the love of her life and Rourke had felt a stab of something akin to jealousy. Which was ridiculous because she was clearly off-limits. He was about to meet twelve beautiful women who were here because they were interested in him. So what if, every time he was in the same room with Portia, his gut knotted and he felt as energized as he did when he was about to close a big deal?

And obviously he hadn't listened closely enough to Nick's pointers. For God's sake, he'd been in her bedroom… But then again, her boyfriend—nah, the love of her life—

"Hello again," said a female voice directly in front of him.

He stopped. He'd almost plowed right into Jacey.

"Sorry, my mind was somewhere else." He shook his head to clear it of Portia. He was delighted Jacey was here. He grinned at her. "It's good to see you. I'm glad you're going to be the person behind the camera on the set."

She returned the grin. "Yeah, it's a regular old home week."

"No kidding. I just ran into Portia," he said.

"Her room is next to mine. We're staying in the servants' quarters," Jacey said. "Tells you something about our jobs, doesn't it?"

"Is it really that bad?" he asked.

"Nah. There are worse ways to make a buck."

"How'd you get started in this business? Have you always been interested in cameras?" he asked, genuinely interested.

Jacey glanced at him suspiciously, as if he couldn't possibly be curious. He laughed aloud at her dark look. "I really want to know. You sort of remind me of my younger brother."

"He's into Goth?"

Rourke laughed aloud at the mental image of Nick decked out in Goth attire. He'd have to be drugged or dead first. "No. He's into Ralph Lauren, but you both say what you think."

Jacey relaxed, and began outlining her work history. The transformation was incredible. Finally, she gave a self-conscious laugh. "Probably more than you bargained for there."

"No. I think that's really cool."

"Have you ever looked through a studio camera?"

"I've never had any exposure to TV before this."

"I could show you sometime. Like maybe after taping or something. If you wanted to. But you don't have to."

"That'd be awesome. I'd love it. You just tell me one day when you have time."

"It's a deal then. The camera brings this clarity to things…" she caught herself. "Whoa, there I go again."

"It's obviously more than a job with you. More like a passion."

"Pretty much." She cocked her dark head to one side and looked at him. "You know, you sort of remind me of Digg. You're real."

"Thanks. I'm extremely flattered. He seems like a great guy." It hadn't been rocket science to figure out that Digg and Jacey were an item. An unlikely item, but an item nonetheless. Although, after chatting with Jacey they didn't seem as unlikely a couple as before.

"He's okay." Her smirk belied her tone. She checked her watch. "Holy shit. You've got a briefing and I've got camera checks in ten minutes. Portia'll have my ass if I'm the reason you're late."

"Really? She's a task master?"

"Not really. But she's punctual."

"She's sort of hard to get to know. What does she do for fun?" Rourke shamelessly pumped Jacey for information about Portia.

"Laundry? Seriously, I don't know. She keeps to herself. Hey, what's with the interest in Portia? Twelve rich girls aren't enough selection for you?"

"Of course not. I mean, of course they are. I was just curious about her since we'll be working together. I'm not interested in her that way."

The minute the words left his mouth, he realized they were patently untrue.

2

"HERE ARE the dossiers on the women you'll be meeting this evening at the predinner cocktail party. You'll find a variety of blondes, brunettes and redheads with varied interests. They do have three things in common. They're all women," Portia joked. Well, only sort of joked. The "female" contestant on *Make Me Over* had surprised everyone when she'd revealed that "she" was a "he." "They're all beautiful and they're all wealthy. You're the most envied man in America."

O'Malley took the booklet and leafed through it.

Portia watched Terry and Jeff, sound techs, check out the wiring and test the sound nearer the divan. They'd planned the meet-and-greet cocktail party in this room. Reminiscent of a Moorish castle, the entire house was a masterpiece of intricate tilework, carved wooden doors, arched doorways and a maze of high-ceilinged hallways that led to private quarters and a central Turkish bath that boasted live palms. The mingled scents of almond, sandalwood, frankincense and myrrh perfumed the air. It was opulent, with more than a hint of decadence, and a most fitting setting for a handsome man and his harem. Actually, and this twist delighted Portia, the house had originally belonged to a 1930s actress infamous for keeping a retinue of lovers on hand, a reversal of the classic male/female harem roles.

This room, the salon, was particularly lavish, with rich fabrics, low sofas, muted lighting and a high ceiling painted to resemble a velvet night sky alight with hundreds of stars. Doubtless these very walls contained the echoes of pleasure, perhaps with more than one lover at a time.

Was it her conversation with Sadie, the sensual setting, or the totally gorgeous bachelor beside her that had forbidden images teasing at the back of her mind? Images of her supine, being pleasured on that low divan by a tall, broad-shouldered, dark-haired man who bore a striking resemblance to O'Malley were inescapable.

Ruthlessly, she swept aside the mental picture. Any pleasure given or received in this room, at least of the carnal nature, wouldn't involve her. Portia's delight would be in the subsequent ratings. One of the twelve women and O'Malley would play out that love scene. And it was her job to see that it happened. Sex sold. Sex pulled in viewers. And ratings meant she'd done her job well.

O'Malley finished thumbing through the photos and bio sheets. "You're right. They're all women." He grinned, which notched up his sex appeal to a devastating level. "They're definitely attractive and they all have that monied look about them. Have you met them? Were they nice? What do you think?"

Portia squashed the tingling response that slid down her spine and reminded herself that Rourke O'Malley was just another pretty face.

She'd met them. *Nice* and *money*, while not mutually exclusive, certainly didn't go hand in hand. Nor did money ensure good taste and decent conduct. All the women had massive egos and she could foresee more than a little jealous bickering. And that would make for good footage. Portia smiled. "I've met them and I think you'll find this very interesting. And very gratifying."

"Good." O'Malley shifted the papers into his other hand. "I know where this question is going to get me, but I've got to ask anyway."

Here it came. The inevitable twist question. The "winner" had been promised her own TV show. It was weird, but hey, it had worked. Any of the women's fathers could probably buy a network, but they all wanted to compete for their own TV show, which should, once again, translate to good footage as they all tried to show how outrageous and at home they could appear on the camera. Of course, she couldn't reveal this to O'Malley. Terry and Jeff moved to the other side of the room, checking the audio cables running along the baseboards. Must be a snafu. She'd better check with them when she wrapped this up with O'Malley. "Go ahead. Ask away."

Anticipating his question and distracted by potential sound problems, she didn't really listen to the question, she just answered what she expected him to ask. "Even if I knew, I couldn't tell you."

He quirked one dark brow. "You can't tell me why you don't like me?"

He'd asked why she didn't like him? A flush crept up her face. Portia had realized early on that one of her greatest assets was her ability to get along well with pretty much anyone and everyone. She had a knack for putting people at ease. People found her easy to talk to. The fact that she never offered personal information in return usually worked to her favor. Mostly people wanted to talk about themselves. "I thought you asked about the twist."

He waved his hand in dismissal. "I never expected that you'd tell me anyway. I know I'm not a virgin, so that's out the window." His blue eyes twinkled devilishly and Portia wasn't sure whether he was making fun of himself or flirting with her, or perhaps both.

But she did know a slow heat seeped through her at the visual supplied by her recently activated imagination—O'Malley naked, thrusting between a woman's naked thighs. "I'm sure. Many times over."

O'Malley shrugged. "*Many* is a relative term. I'm not a player. And I can only hope you don't slip in a transvestite like on that other show." He grinned, and Portia smiled in return. Most drop-dead gorgeous men took themselves far more seriously than O'Malley.

"No surprises there." The production crew had managed to save that show, but afterward the executive director, Burt Mueller, threatened to can the

entire screening crew if another transvestite revealed him- or herself on one of his shows. In typical Burt Mueller fashion, he'd declared he
wouldn't become known as the Transvestite Forum
Network. She reassured Rourke again. "They're all
real women."

"For certain?"

"For certain."

"That's good to know," he said.

She bet it was. Portia'd seen a few looks pass between some of the male crew that clearly said they
didn't want to think about the point when a guy
might figure out the "woman" carried the same
equipment they did.

"You still haven't answered my question. Why
don't you like me?" Despite his easy smile, his eyes
were serious.

"I don't dislike you." And she didn't. Not exactly.
She was wary. When he'd been on the set of *The Last
Virgin*, she'd dismissed him, categorizing him the
way she did all narcissistic men. But O'Malley refused to be dismissed or categorized and that wasn't
a good thing. His low-key charm and good looks
raised Portia's red flags. It was akin to instinctively
knowing a pretty red berry you found in the woods
might look good and taste good but wasn't necessarily good for you. However, she was supposed to be
working with him and keeping him happy. She reiterated her earlier assertion. "I don't dislike you at
all."

"I think you're splitting hairs."

O'Malley was more discerning than she'd given

him credit. "I have a job to do. I can't allow myself to get too close to our cast members."

"I just feel like you know everything about me and I know nothing about you."

She shook her head. "Contestants pretty much agree to open their lives up to the public. It's the price of celebrity. But there's the difference. You're a participant. I'm behind the scenes. And I like it that way." She personally thought anyone who agreed to come on to one of these shows wasn't dealing with a full deck anyway, which was statistically frightening when you considered the staggering number of applicants flooding the screening sites. Andrea and Zach from *The Last Virgin* had been exceptions. She'd heard through the studio grapevine that Sarah Donovan and Luke Richards from *Surviving Sarah* and Charlie Cuesta and Sam Ryan from *The Great Chase* weren't flakes either. Thank goodness, though, for all those other quirky people in the world because it meant she had a job.

"You're here for a love fest. I'm here to make sure it goes well for you. End of story." She smiled, but they both knew she meant it.

Honestly, if she hadn't known better, she'd swear hurt flashed in his eyes before he answered her smile with his own. "You're absolutely right. I apologize for overstepping boundaries."

Now she felt even more awkward, as if she'd extracted an apology that wasn't owed. "Don't worry about it." She checked her watch, relieved to see it was time to end this. "Okay, I should let you get back to your room to shower and change."

How many times had she said that to a man in similar circumstances and never thought a thing about it? What was wrong with her that she suddenly had a disturbingly erotic image of O'Malley naked, dripping wet, surrounded by a thick cloud of steam? And found it totally, inappropriately arousing.

She glanced back down at the clipboard in her hands, not because there was anything important there, but because it gave her somewhere to look other than at him. "Wardrobe will be along to your room in an hour or so. And I'll meet you there in an hour and a half to go over any last-minute questions."

O'Malley's smile held an edge. "Ah, yes, so you can expertly orchestrate my—what was it?—love fest." He gave her a nod of dismissal and walked away.

Portia stood in the middle of the room and watched his broad-shouldered retreat, until the door closed behind him.

"So, are you the newest member of the fan club, Portia?" Terry called from across the room, his voice teasing.

Startled, she almost dropped her clipboard. Damn, she'd been so caught up in watching him walk across the room, she'd forgotten about Terry and Jeff.

"You boys know better than that. I don't do fan clubs."

Bottom line. She orchestrated. He participated. And that was that.

"HOLD STILL for one more second..." Cindy from wardrobe tugged his black tie into place. She stepped back and surveyed him with a critical eye. A knock sounded on his bedroom door.

"Come in," he called over his shoulder. Portia had said she'd arrive in an hour and a half. She was punctual. Behind him, his bedroom door opened and closed.

He knew without turning that it was Portia. Yeah, she was scheduled to be here, but he could feel her. Tiny hairs stood up on the back of his neck and adrenaline surged through him.

Cindy tweaked his tux jacket and smiled. "Your mama will be proud and those women don't stand a chance." Cindy, with her cheerful attitude and nonstop chatter, rather reminded him of his mother. "Honey, you are yum-my." She winked outrageously at him and looked over his shoulder. "Makes you wish you had a spoon so you could eat him up doesn't it?"

Laughing—how could you not laugh at such outrageous hyperbole—and she was obviously teasing him rather than flirting—he turned to face Portia.

Her answering smile struck him as a bit forced. "He's lucky I left my spoon in my room."

Her cool gaze flickered over him, having just the opposite effect on his temperature. Forget a spoon, he mentally urged her. His body tightened and his heart pounded at the thought of her mouth against his skin, her scent mingling with his. What was it about her that drew him to her? She wasn't beautiful in the accepted sense of the word, but she was arresting, exotic, intriguing, frustrating—and she got under his skin.

Cindy's two-way radio went off. Tamsin, the lead makeup artist, came across after the initial squawk. "Cindy, Ms. Freeman needs you ASAP."

Rourke had skimmed through the dossiers again, after his shower and before Cindy arrived. Lissa Freeman was heiress to a mind-boggling real-estate fortune, who'd spent the last year hanging out in Europe. What the dossier didn't include, but the media had more than adequately covered, was the havoc Lissa had wrecked along the way. She was a dark-haired, petulant time bomb given to explosions when things didn't go her way. Of course, he as well as anyone knew you couldn't and shouldn't believe all the media hype.

The radio clicked again. "I don't need you ASAP, I needed you five minutes ago."

Okay. Maybe you could believe the media. That peremptory tone could only belong to Ms. Freeman.

Cindy headed for the door, smirking. "Bet she doesn't have a clue you heard _that_. Bet she'll use a different tone with you."

Rourke chuckled. "No doubt."

The radio clicked again. "Are you on your way? I don't have all night."

"Okay, I can't resist and she deserves it," Cindy said to Rourke and Portia. She clicked the two-way. "I'm almost finished with Mr. O'Malley and then I'll be right there."

"Oh. Take your time. There's no hurry." Butter

wouldn't have melted in Lissa Freeman's mouth this time around.

Cindy laughed and shook her head. "Take care of him," she said to Portia. "We're putting a guppy into a tank full of sharks."

A guppy? He laughed to cover his sudden nervousness. Him, patently incapable of small talk, among twelve socially adept women. Right. "I object to being called a guppy."

Cindy waved her radio. "You know what I mean. Take care of him, Portia."

"I have the utmost confidence he'll be fine," Portia said. He was glad one of them did.

The minute the door closed behind Cindy the mood shifted and Rourke was aware of being in his bedroom alone with Portia Tomlinson, a woman he found both bewitching and aggravating.

He was aware of the bed with its massive carved headboard and gossamer curtains tied back with silken cords, the lush carpet underfoot, the sensual suggestion of the entwined couple in the gilt-framed reproduction of Gustav Klimt's "The Kiss" adorning the wall, the copy of the *Kama Sutra* on the bedside table, the muted lighting, the sheer elegance of Portia's upswept blond hair, her no-nonsense suit paired with sexy designer shoes, and most of all, her scent.

Rourke spoke to fill the space with something other than the sexual tension strumming through him and permeating the room. "Lissa Freeman just narrowed my choices down to eleven."

"You should meet her with an open mind. She's

probably got a bad case of PDS, predate syndrome," Portia said.

"Would you talk to someone like that even if you were nervous over a date?"

"No. Probably not, but you should still give her another chance."

What would Portia be like on a date? Cool and reserved? What did she do for fun? To relax? What excited her?

"Okay," her voice came out low and husky. She stopped and cleared her throat. Maybe she was as affected by him as he was by her. "So, we should go over any last-minute questions you have."

Rourke tried to focus on the women he was about to meet instead of the one in front of him, but he was totally captivated by the way the shadows played across Portia's skin and hair. He reminded himself the real purpose of being here was not to admire the straight line of Portia's nose or the sensual curve of her mouth, but to give the network their show, pick up his prize money, and keep Nick's butt out of jail. "Do you have any pointers on tonight?"

"Only one, really. We've set up a champagne fountain in the salon. You might want to go easy on it since you're the star."

"Not a problem. I'm not a big drinker." Some of the guys on the set of *The Last Virgin* had complained about the minimal alcohol served. "Why didn't we have a champagne fountain on the last set?"

"This is a different show altogether and the dynamics have shifted. Sexist or not, alcohol flowing freely among lots of men and one woman just doesn't work. But you know sex sells the ratings. You're a sexy man and they're beautiful women, so Lauchmann ordered champagne to loosen things up."

"I manage fine without 'loosening up my dates' with alcohol," he said, just to set the record straight. Then he moved on to her comment that had caught and held his attention. "You think I'm sexy?"

"Of course I do." Her expression remained pleasant and neutral, making him all the more curious as to what was going on in her head. "And that really doesn't mean anything. I consider a Ferrari a work of art. I can admire it, but it doesn't mean I want to drive one."

He didn't need to be a rocket scientist to know this conversation was about much more than a car. And he knew he was going where he shouldn't, but he went there anyway. "What if you were offered a test drive?"

"They only want you to drive if you're interested in buying, and I can't afford a Ferrari."

"What if it was a no-strings-attached test drive?"

"I'd pass. It would only make me want what I know I can't have. I'm a realist."

So was he, but he also had dreams, fantasies. Somewhere beneath that cool cover, surely she had fantasies as well. "And what is it about the Ferrari that appeals to you?"

"The same thing that appeals to everyone else. Beautiful, sexy lines. Perfectly proportioned. Responsive. I've read that it shifts hard and fast, but smooth. All of that power under the hood." Her eyes glittered. "All the women you're about to meet can afford Ferraris, probably more than one."

What exactly were the rules of engagement? And what did it take to shake her up the way she shook him up inside? "What if I want to bring one back to my room?"

"I don't think a Ferrari will fit in here."

So she wasn't shaken, but she did have a sense of humor. "I was asking more along the lines of one of the women."

Portia looked pointedly at the large bed. "That's certainly your prerogative. I believe there's room for all twelve. And of course there aren't any cameras in here."

"How can I be sure there isn't a Minicam with a microphone tucked away somewhere?"

"Because I'm telling you there isn't. You'll just have to trust me on this."

Given the studio's twist on the last show, parading Andrea Scarpini before the world as the last virgin, he'd be a fool to trust the studio or anyone associated with the studio. "So, if I want to bring one of them back here for…privacy…it's okay?"

She glanced toward the bed. "Absolutely."

"And if I bring back a different woman every night?"

"A different one every night or more than one, it's up to you." Ah, she could play the part of cool and collected, but the flush that suffused her neck and face was all too telling. She walked over to the nightstand and opened it. Rourke did a double take. The drawer held several boxes of condoms. "We take your welfare very seriously. If you find you're running low, just let me know."

This was worse than when his parents had put a brown-paper bag filled with condoms in the medicine cabinet when he was in high school and told him it was better to be safe than sorry.

Rourke laughed, both amused and offended. So much for needling Portia to get a rise out of her. He hadn't signed on for stud service. "I think that's an adequate supply." Hell, he hadn't run through that many condoms in a lifetime. And twice when he was working out at the gym, his back had gone out. Running through that many condoms would probably put him in traction.

"The only rule is everyone has to be willing. *No* means *no*."

"And does that no work both ways? What if one of them comes on to me and I'm not interested?"

"I suppose you'd handle it much the same as you would on a date at home."

"Maybe. But at home, I'd have the option of just not calling her again."

"Don't forget you'll be eliminating contestants. Of course, it won't be as many or as often as it was on *The Last Virgin*, because we're starting out with fewer people."

"And what if I don't want to kiss any of them?"

Her smile held a tight edge. "I find that scenario unlikely. Surely out of a dozen beautiful women, you'll be attracted to at least one." She glanced down at her clipboard. "I can't imagine you won't be inspired to share a few kisses at the Turkish bath or on the terrace."

"Doesn't it make you uncomfortable? Watching people kiss? Listening to intimate conversation?" Rourke had always been very private and Portia seemed so reserved, he couldn't imagine it didn't make her uncomfortable. God, his palms were sweating just thinking about facing a dozen women, much less making out with them.

She shrugged. "We're doing a job. You distance yourself. It helps if you think of yourself as an actor playing a part."

"I don't suppose you're willing to tell me where there aren't any cameras other than here?"

"No, I'm afraid I can't do that. It's cheating, plus it would cheat our viewers at home."

"Do you always play by the rules, Portia?" He knew the answer before he asked.

"Absolutely. Do you?" she challenged back.

"I always have before. I've never wanted something so much that I was willing to break the rules for it, but if I wanted something—" he looked into the depths of her eyes and paused deliberately "—or someone, desperately, if I couldn't think of anything else…"

"That sounds obsessive." A husky note colored her voice.

"I think it's that same fine line that separates love and hate," he said.

She deliberately looked away from him, breaking the tenuous sensual thread woven by their conversation. "Well, let's go meet your bachelorettes and see if you find a woman who inspires you to break the rules."

3

"YOU SEEM nervous," Portia said to Rourke outside the salon. He might be nervous, but she was relieved to be out of his bedroom and away from that big bed and assortment of condoms.

"Hell, yeah, I'm nervous."

This didn't seem like a playboy to her. "Don't be. They're just women and you're absolutely gorgeous. They'll be falling all over themselves to get to you." She offered the same reassurances that were part of her stock in trade. Ridiculous, really, what an abhorrent thought it was this time.

The set of his shoulders, beneath the dark jacket and crisp white shirt of his tux, was definitely tense. "Turn around and hold this." She handed him her clipboard. Taking a deep breath herself, she lightly massaged his shoulders. She'd never actually done this for any other contestants, but certainly she would have if she'd thought they needed it. It had nothing to do with actually wanting to touch O'Malley because she didn't. She didn't *want* to touch him, didn't want to feel the hard muscles beneath her fingertips. This was nothing personal, this was just her job.

"Where did you learn to do that?" he asked with a low moan of appreciation.

"I've always been good with my hands."

"Oh, Portia."

It took no imagination to hear that voice moaning her name in bed, her hands on something other than his shoulders... What was wrong with her? Was it the conversation with Sadie? The conversation with O'Malley with its deeper level of meaning? The sensual setting? *Easy, Portia, girl. Get yourself in check.*

"You'll be fine," she said as she smoothed out his jacket. She dropped her hands to her sides.

Pivoting slowly until he faced her, his eyes dark, serious, he bent his head until he was so close she felt the warmth of his breath against her face, and could see the fine lines bracketing his eyes. Oh, God, O'Malley was going to kiss her. And the worst of it was, she wanted it. She wanted to feel his mouth on hers, to test the texture of his lips, to sample in his kiss the heat reflected in his eyes. "Portia..."

At the very last second, sanity prevailed. What was she thinking? Anyone could walk by. Any crew member. And what was he thinking? Did he assume he was such a hot commodity that any woman was fair game? She stepped away.

She took her clipboard from him and prayed he didn't see her hands shaking. She checked the schedule she'd already memorized and glanced at her watch. "Thirty seconds and you're on."

He reached as if to brush his fingers over her

cheekbone and longing coursed through her, so intense it nearly buckled her knees. How long since she'd shivered with the heat of a man's touch? How long had she denied herself as a woman? And this was absolutely the wrong man to feel this way with. At the last minute he pulled back and let his hand fall.

Portia licked her dry lips. "It's time for you to go inside."

He shook his head, as if he'd lost track of reality as well. He looked oddly vulnerable and unsure of himself. "I'm—"

"Ready to meet your ladies," she finished for him, still quaking inside from that near kiss. She had to get them both back on track. "Viewers already love you and these women will too."

Portia turned on the mike that fed directly into the earpiece of Grant Atwood, the show's emcee. "Ten seconds to showtime." She mentally counted backward. Reaching the number one, she opened the door and sent Rourke in, stepping aside so that the camera wouldn't pick her up in the background. O'Malley moved into the room as if he owned it.

Portia had thought all the women were lovely before, but tonight, they were positively stunning. Money couldn't buy happiness, and according to the show's title it didn't buy love, but money certainly bought some kick-butt outfits. Two gowns screamed signature Versace, as well as Vera Wang, Halston and what looked like a Dolce and Gabbana. And the shoes and the jewelry were spectacular.

There was more money tied up in those dresses than she made in a year. Make that a couple of years. Not to mention the accessories. And she'd bet there wasn't a rhinestone on the property. Tara Mitchells wore a pair of Jimmy Choos with a diamond mesh collar that wrapped around the ankle. Paste didn't sparkle like that. Portia's finely cut suit had seemed perfectly presentable...until now. These women were glitz, glamour and designer fashion at its finest and the audience would eat it up. And O'Malley should too, she thought with a hint of cattiness as the women all preened before him.

Grant started the introductions. Portia found a dark corner and observed. Each woman had been instructed not to kiss O'Malley. From a practical standpoint, they didn't need to have their star covered in lipstick and it also gave O'Malley the position of authority. It was all about playing up the harem aspect.

Jacey's camera was rolling and Portia couldn't have asked for a better round of first filming. Despite his earlier pre-entry tension, O'Malley was perfect, greeting each woman as if he were truly glad to meet her, brushing his lips against her cheek as if it were a prelude or a promise of more to come. She knew what it felt like to have his warm breath feather against her skin, to be enveloped in his dark, spicy scent, to feel anticipation quiver through her. But she didn't know what it felt like to have his lips caress her flesh. And thinking this way was sheer, utter madness. Hadn't she just told him that the crew distanced themselves? And whatever this thing, this tension, between herself and O'Malley, surely it would dissipate with the arrival of his women, wouldn't it? Whatever it was that simmered between them was probably just a product of all the hype and the sexual tension conjured up by the situation and the setting. Now he had not just another, but a dozen other outlets for his interest and that suited her just fine. Didn't it?

"I DIDN'T THINK it was possible, but you're even better-looking in person," Carlotta Zimmerman said. Carlotta was the last of the twelve.

Rourke laughed. "Thanks. It's the tux. Even Yoda would look good in a tux."

Carlotta smiled rather blankly, obviously missing the *Star Wars* reference. Oh, well. He bent and pressed a light kiss to her cheek, the same as he had eleven times before. "Thank you for being here. It's an honor to meet you."

Carlotta turned to join the crowd. They were all beautiful. They all smelled good. Looked good. It had actually gone better than he'd anticipated, but he hadn't felt any rush of sexual energy, no slow ribbon of desire curling through him the way he had in the hallway with Portia. She was tucked in the far-left corner now. He'd been excruciatingly aware of her quiet circumnavigation of the room. In her plain suit, with her hair in the twist she favored, she embodied understated elegance and poise. The other women looked almost garish in comparison.

A waiter offered him a flute of champagne from

a tray. He snagged one, sipping. It wasn't his favorite beverage, but it was cold and wet and quite frankly he wouldn't mind a little bit of alcohol to take the edge off, although he wasn't nearly as nervous as he had been. Now he had a half hour of mix and mingle.

He had to admit, being the center of all this female attention was pretty flattering. Of course, he didn't know any man who wouldn't be flattered by this. Maybe he didn't need Nick's prescribed therapy after all. Maybe this was therapy. Maybe now he wouldn't make a fool of himself the next time he was with Portia and do something stupid like try to kiss her.

"Rourke, why don't you propose a toast?" Lissa Freeman said, curling her arm through his and pressing against his side, as if they were already an item. Lissa's full breasts pressed against his jacketed arm. Oddly, her barely clad bosom didn't send a jolt through him the way Portia's hands on his shoulders had.

A redhead—he couldn't remember her name— slid in front of Tara Mitchells and positioned herself on his other side. Okay, so these two were definitely the most aggressive of the pack. If he remembered correctly, an explicit tape featuring the redhead and her boyfriend du jour had surfaced on the Internet last year. Rourke had passed on watching it, but Jason, two offices down, had gone into a serious state of lust, and would definitely freak when this show aired. The other women surrounded him and he almost laughed as he recalled

Cindy from wardrobe's earlier shark analogy. They were all dressed to kill.

They all looked at him expectantly. He'd better get on with a toast and quit making bad jokes to himself.

Smiling, he raised his glass. "Here's to a successful show and to all you lovely ladies."

They all touched their glasses to each others' and drank. Rourke tried to sip from his, but it was damn hard to drink without spilling with Lissa attached to his arm like a limpet.

"Now, *I'd* like to propose a toast," the limpet said. She looked at him. "Here's to the beginning of a beautiful relationship."

Well, hell, he'd drink to that as long as it didn't include her, and she hadn't been specific. No sooner had he lowered his glass than the redhead—Maggie, that was her name—not to be outdone by Lissa, piped up. "My turn. Here's to hoping the camera gets us at our best angle."

Apparently now it had turned into a game because Bridget Anders, another contestant, waved the champagne-laden waiter over. "I've got one." Everyone refreshed their glasses. "To long hot nights."

Rourke lost track of who proposed what. He simply raised his glass, laughing as the toasts got progressively more suggestive.

At one point someone actually grabbed his butt and copped a feel. He worked very hard to relax and go with the flow of being the center of attention among very flirtatious, aggressive, beautiful women, but throughout it all, he was always aware of where Portia was in the room. He was, he reminded himself, an actor, but he felt as if he were playing for an audience of one.

PORTIA DRIED OFF and pulled on her terry-cloth robe, hurrying to free up the space. Servants' quarters didn't come with en suite bathrooms and there were six other crew members on site. She gathered her toiletries and knocked as she passed Jacey's room. "It's all yours," she called out.

She heard Jacey's muffled thanks.

Portia closed herself into her bedroom. The past several days on the set had been long and draining. And that hadn't been, she assured herself as she pulled on the shorts and T-shirt that doubled for pajama duty, because she'd had to watch a dozen women cover O'Malley like bees on a honeycomb. That was, after all, why they were here. There were myriad details that had to be overseen each day, and O'Malley was merely one of them. It had nothing to do with the fact that she tossed and turned, exhausted but restless, dreaming disturbing erotic dreams that recapped the days' events but put her center-stage with O'Malley. Small wonder, then, that after a night spent dreaming about him, it felt as if every flirtatious glance, every shared joke, every light-and-easy kiss he exchanged with the contestants was, in fact, meant for her. She'd heard about this happening—being locked on location and losing touch with reality. She could deal with it, of course, but she was becoming mentally and emotionally exhausted.

Even her hard, narrow bed looked welcoming about now. She towel-dried her wet hair. That was the benefit of straight hair and a good conditioner, she didn't have to blow-dry. She'd just brush it and stick it in a twist tomorrow and she'd be set.

She turned down the covers and was just slipping between the sheets when her pager went off. Damnation. What now?

O'Malley. What could he possibly want this close to midnight? Hadn't he had enough attention with all the fawning earlier tonight? She wasn't a night person. She was tired and cranky and he was cutting into *her* time, although as long as they were on location, she was, in effect, on duty 24/7. But she'd had enough of O'Malley for the day. Enough of his dark good looks, his easy charm, even that scent of his that seemed to invade her space when he was around. And she'd definitely had enough of feeling as if she was walking on eggshells.

"What's up, O'Malley?" she asked without preamble. Oy, that was the wrong thing to ask a man who'd just spent three hours with a dozen hot women. "What do you need?" Possibly not the best wording either. Dammit. She gave up.

"I can't…um…get up," he said in a low, strained voice.

She'd have bet her knock-off Prada bag that *that* wouldn't be a problem for him. It was sort of disappointing to learn and sort of gross, too. "I don't need to hear this."

He laughed, still low and strained. "I didn't say

I couldn't get *it* up. You don't understand. I can't get up. Literally. I need your help."

"Why can't you get up?"

"What? You think I want to humiliate myself and call you, be a pain in the ass late at night? No. But I can't shoot tomorrow if I'm stuck, now can I?"

Blast. She'd been so relieved he wasn't confessing impotence, she'd missed the filming implication.

"Where are you now?" she asked.

"On the floor in my room."

"What—" Never mind. She find out soon enough. "I'll be right there."

"Thanks."

Because it was business all day, every day, she had work clothes and more work clothes. Somehow putting on a suit to go rescue O'Malley seemed sort of dumb. What the hell? Like he couldn't handle her in running shorts and a T-shirt? She slid her feet into flip-flops and closed her bedroom door behind her. She passed the bathroom and heard Jacey singing in the shower. Portia grinned to herself. Who would've figured Jacey for a shower crooner? You just never knew. Or maybe she was just under the influence of love. She and Digg were openly an item now. They'd met on the set of *Killing Time* last year. Digg had been a contestant and Jacey was the lead camera. According to the rumor mill, Jacey'd been fired for about half an hour and Digg had damn near got himself kicked off the show. Contestant/crew fraternization wasn't the slickest move for either one of them to make. It had almost cost Digg a million bucks and Jacey her job and reputation.

Navigating the maze of hallways, which were kind of spooky late at night, Portia made a mental note to remember what had happened with Jacey and Digg. Letting herself into O'Malley's room, she stifled a laugh. O'Malley was on the floor, folded over like an envelope.

"You should lock your door."

"I forgot. It's a good thing I did or you couldn't have gotten in."

"I'm scared to ask, but exactly what were you doing?"

"Exercising." He turned his head to look at her. "You know you're dead if you laugh."

It had to be fairly uncomfortable folded over that way, but O'Malley had a devilish twinkle in his blue eyes.

"You don't look particularly dangerous to me."

"Ah, but sooner or later I'll be mobile again."

Okay, so maybe she'd been a bit hasty labeling him safe. Now that she wasn't suffering the heebie-jeebies from the dark hallway and had sort of figured out what was going on with O'Malley, she noticed he was wearing pajama bottoms. And nothing else.

Holy mother of God, his back was spectacular, a physical work of art. All the saliva in her mouth evaporated as heat rushed through her like a wildfire.

She ran her tongue over her dry lips. "How can I help you? I'm not a doctor."

"This has happened twice before at the gym. The trainer got behind me and sort of pulled, slow and steady."

"Okay." Portia moved behind him and swallowed hard. If he'd looked good from the doorway he was positively...orgasmic up close. The light from the bedside lamp spilled across him, burnishing his skin with a golden glow.

"If you can, straddle me and slip your arms under mine."

She braced her feet on either side of his hips and leaned down, hooking her arms beneath his armpits. He was hurt and she was helping, but, God help her, it felt wonderfully intimate to touch the satin of his skin, to smell his scent, to feel the brush of his pajama-clad hips against her bare legs.

"Don't try to pick me up. Just move forward a bit and then straighten me up."

Portia froze, her arms wrapped around his muscular torso, her face near his dark hair, her bra-free breasts precariously close to his muscular back. "I've never done this before. What if I don't do it right?" Not only would she feel bad for hurting O'Malley, but crippling the star wouldn't exactly go over big with her bosses, Lauchmann and Mueller. "I think we should call a doctor."

She untangled herself from him and discovered she could actually breathe again.

"No doctor. You're one of the most efficient people I've ever met. I trust you. This time try linking your hands, just to get a little more leverage."

Once again she wrapped her arms around him

from behind. She linked her hands as he'd instructed and pressed them against his broad chest. Masculine hair teased her fingers.

Portia was suddenly, poignantly aware that she hadn't had sex in ten, long, dry years and her nipples were in hard, intimate contact with his back. Thank you, sex drive, for some spectacularly bad timing.

"That's it," he said, his voice more strained than ever.

He must be hurting to suddenly sound so strained, and here she was dithering like a sex-starved idiot. Wait. She *was* sex-starved, only she hadn't realized it until now because suddenly, around O'Malley, all she could think of was sex.

His heart pounded against her hand like a sledgehammer. He'd put his trust in her and she'd help him get some relief. Bracing herself, she tugged forward and then slowly pulled him into an upright sitting position.

"Uh, I need to lie down if you can sort of let go."

Mortified that she'd been standing there pressed against him, she immediately released him and stepped away, putting several feet between them. She was so wickedly strung out just from touching him that the whole distance of the house didn't even seem safe.

"So, you're okay now?" she asked, backing toward the door, desperate to escape O'Malley's appeal.

"I'm sorry to ask, but I need to ice it now." He cautiously climbed on the bed and lay flat on his belly. "There's a fridge over by the sofa, cleverly disguised as an end table. There's some ice in there."

Talk about stark contrasts between her room and his, from communal bath to in-room fridge. She crossed the room to the divan he'd referred to as a couch. Sure enough, the table was actually a fridge. She pulled out the modest ice supply. "Got any plastic bags lying around?"

"There was one but they picked my laundry up in it earlier."

"Hold on a second."

"I'm not going anywhere," he said dryly from his supine position on the bed.

Portia went into the bathroom and looked around. O'Malley's shaving gear, deodorant, toothbrush, and comb were strewn over the bathroom counter, but there were no bags. O'Malley was no neatnik, that was for sure. She grabbed a hand towel.

She had a plastic bag back in her room but that meant going out into that dark hallway two more times than was absolutely necessary. Probably either the kitchen or the laundry center had plastic bags but that also meant wandering around this place in the middle of the night, no thanks, or rousing some of the house staff and that seemed very thoughtless.

She walked back into the bedroom. Come on, she was resourceful. Think. Maybe the bedside table. She pulled opened the drawer and rooted around. No, nothing but a wide assortment of rubbers. She slammed the drawer shut. Whoa. Nah. Sure. Why not? If he ran out, she'd replace them. She reopened the drawer and pulled out a condom.

"Oh, my God, Portia, this is like a fantasy come true," Rourke began in a choked voice, "but I'm not sure I'm up to this. Wait. What the hell am I saying? The sexiest woman in the universe is standing next to my bed unwrapping a condom. Hell, yes, I'm up to it. I just need to roll onto my back, but you'll have to do most of the work."

It took her hormonally oversaturated brain about a nanosecond to fill in those blanks and imagine herself peeling off her clothes, ripping off his pajamas and climbing on and going for a ride. No, no and no!

"I'm making you an icepack. For your back."

"Oh." He lay there for a second with his eyes closed, then reopened them. "Now would be a good time for a Vulcan mind meld, so I could erase what I just said. As if it wasn't humiliating enough for you to find me that way."

"Unfortunately for you, a true Vulcan mind meld would give me total access to your thoughts and memories." Dear God, he'd called her the sexiest woman in the universe. The comment went right to her head and all of her other severely neglected womanly parts.

Without thinking she blew gently into the condom to open it. O'Malley watched her and it wasn't pain reflected in his eyes.

It was suddenly incredibly hot in his room. As if a furnace had been cranked, her internal heater was out of control. She packed ice into the penis-shaped rubber. She held it in one hand and put the ice in with the other. Her hand was warm, the ice was cold, and it became increasingly difficult to keep it under control. Damn, why'd she pick a lubricated one?

"Okay, I've already forfeited all my pride today, so I'll just confess that I can't watch you do that." He closed his eyes and immediately popped them open again. "Or, let's just say that I shouldn't."

She should turn her back, go into the bathroom, do anything other than what she was doing. If she were a heroine in a romance novel or a made-for-TV movie, she'd be written right out of the script for standing there and teasing him with her deliberate stroking movements. She'd left her brain somewhere, maybe in that spooky hall. The sexual energy pulsing between them made her feel almost drunk.

"You are a wicked woman, Portia Tomlinson. I think you have a sadistic streak."

"You're watching. Does that mean you're a masochist?"

"That's a distinct possibility where you're concerned."

She tied off the end of the icy phallus. She'd always known that the summer she'd worked kids' birthday parties as a clown and tied a gazillion balloons would come in handy one day.

She admired her handiwork. "Seems a shame to waste it, but I understand you're in pain. I guess I'm willing to make a sacrifice. Where does it hurt?"

"You don't really want to know, so why don't we settle on my lower back?"

Laughing, she wrapped the ice-packed condom in the hand towel and knelt on the edge of the bed. She placed the bundle right above the drawstring waist of his pajamas. "How's that?"

"It's lower."

She scooted the hand towel against his pajamas, pushing the material down. Actually touching him didn't seem like the brightest move. "How's that?"

"No. A little lower."

She pushed lower still and only found bare skin. "That's it. Right there."

No elastic band indicated boxers or jockeys, which meant no underwear. Just awesome man beneath those thin cotton bottoms. Suddenly it wasn't so funny. Suddenly it was hard to breathe, hard to look anywhere but at the expanse of gorgeous man-skin in front of her. And suddenly he wasn't just another pretty boy in Hollywood, he was O'Malley who wanted Vulcan mind melts to make her forget he thought she was the sexiest woman in the universe. It would be so easy to go with his misinterpretation. She could open another condom, roll him onto his back, touch him until he was aroused and then she could slide on top of him, take him inside her where she throbbed with an ache he'd started, and stay there until they were both satisfied…. She jumped off the bed like a scalded cat.

"Goodnight," she said, rooted to the spot. The sane portion of her urged her toward the door and sanity. The insane portion held her immobile, drinking in the sight of a sexy, half-naked O'Malley sprawled on silk sheets.

"Thank you. For everything." O'Malley said. "Is it true?" he asked, pointing to her T-shirt.

"What?" Portia instinctively glanced at I Love Nerds printed on the front of her shirt. Danny had given her the shirt for Valentine's Day. Trekkie, Harry Potter addict and fledgling mad scientist, her son took great pride in being a self-professed nerd. "Yeah. My…a friend gave it to me. I do love nerds. I adore them. I live with one."

"I see." The light in his eyes died.

"O'Malley, as far as we're both concerned, none of this ever happened."

Portia scrambled for the door. Nothing in those dark, labyrinthine hallways could possibly be as frightening as the things O'Malley made her want.

4

THE FOLLOWING MORNING Rourke presented himself on the terrace at precisely nine o'clock. He hadn't slept worth a damn last night; instead he'd wasted his time replaying his moment of humiliation when he'd revealed to Portia how eager he was to have her in his bed, torturing himself with the memory of her hands on his bare skin, the press of her breasts against his back, and trying to fit together the different pieces of the puzzle that comprised this fascinating woman. And taking heart in the knowledge that she wasn't immune to him either.

She sat at the far end of the terrace where the brilliant California sun wasn't impeded by the vine-laden pergola that cast a diamond pattern over the stone floor. He headed toward her, passing the mosaic fountain that burbled soothingly in the middle of the sun-dappled terrace.

Portia looked up from the notes she was making on her clipboard and offered a bright, impersonal smile. "Good morning. Thank you for being so punctual." He'd noticed over the last several days, much as on *The Last Virgin* set, that she worked hard, possessed infinite patience and was *always* on time.

If today was anything like the rest of the week, having a moment alone with Portia without wardrobe, camera and sound people around would be scarce after their morning briefing. He took advantage of the temporary privacy.

"About last night—"

"You handled yourself beautifully at dinner," Portia interrupted. "Just the right amount of attention to each woman. Have you made a decision?" She smiled and nursed a cup of tea, pleasant and neutral. Obviously the last night he was talking about—that she *knew* he was talking about—was not up for discussion.

Dressed in a suit, her hair in its signature twist, last night truly could have never happened. But it had—even if she was determined to pretend it hadn't. Unfortunately, no Vulcan could save him from his memories of her in his room with her hair hanging about her face in damp strands, sexy and disheveled in shorts and a T-shirt.

He'd been a long way from handling himself beautifully last night. He'd made a total fool of himself. When he'd looked up and seen her opening that condom…it had been like winning the lottery. It had been a moment of revelation, a revelation of how much he wanted her rather than the women he was supposed to choose from.

"Have you thought about who you want to eliminate?" she prompted him again, pulling him out of his thoughts.

That was easy enough. "Lissa Freeman."

She opened her mouth, a slight frown tugging at

her blond brows and he preempted her. "I'm sure about Lissa and it's not because of the walkie-talkie thing the first day or the fact that she superglues herself to me like a permanent fixture every chance she gets." Rourke gazed past Portia to the spectacular canyon view and the exclusive homes dotting the hillside. "She's made several catty comments to and about the other women. I don't have time for people who feel good about themselves at the expense of someone else." He turned his back to the view and faced Portia, the sun warm against his neck and shoulders. Her scent drifted to him, around him.

"Then Lissa's out." Portia eyed him over her cup rim. "She really pushed your button, didn't she?"

Rourke shoved his hands into his pockets. "I was the someone else more times than I care to recall in junior high and high school." What the hell? Why not tell her? It wasn't as if he could humiliate himself any more than he already had last night.

She raised one delicate eyebrow. "I find that hard to believe."

He shrugged. "My nickname in high school was Rourke the Dork."

"Why would anyone call *you* that?"

"Because it rhymes?" Feeling extremely self-conscious and regretting having brought it up, he leaned against the thick arbor post covered in ropey vines. "I was tall and skinny with pop-bottle glasses and braces to correct a serious overbite. I was a dork, and I knew I was a dork. But I didn't need it pointed out in the hallway or at the lockers."

"That couldn't have felt good." Her voice held a soft note.

Great. He didn't want to be some object of pity. "That was then. The best revenge is living well and—" he gestured to the view beyond them "—here I am." It made a good cover for being here on Nick's behalf.

She nodded. "With twelve, make that eleven, of the world's most beautiful, wealthy women clamoring for you."

"The dork's revenge."

"Well, you're certainly not a dork any longer." For a second he glimpsed heat beneath her ever-present reserve, sending a prickle of awareness through him. A breeze rustled the leaves overhead and teased a few strands of hair about her cheek.

"Sure I am. The outside may have changed a little, but I'm still the same inside. And that's not a problem for me. I'm fine being a dork." He really didn't want to talk about this any more. He dropped into a chair opposite Portia. "Okay, so Lissa's out of here…"

Portia made a note on her clipboard. "This is a little different from the last show. We'll gather all the contestants together and then you have to tell her."

He winced. "That's not a problem with Lissa, but this is going to get harder and harder. Most of them seem like nice women."

"That's great that you feel that way. Is there anyone in particular you feel like you really clicked with?"

You. But he knew as well as he knew his own name that particular answer would send her running out the door, the same way it had last night.

"It's still early yet for that."

"You're not making my job any easier." Her laugh washed over him like a cool brook beneath the warm sun. "There's no one you'd like to get to know better? Find out what really makes her tick?"

His heart thudded heavily in his chest as he looked into her eyes, telling her what he wouldn't voice. *You. I want to know you inside and out.*

"By *better* do you mean her favorite color? The taste of her skin? Her preferred ice cream flavor? The way she looks when she's just waking up and still drowsy? Whether she likes lazy afternoons with a crossword puzzle in front of a fire or a trip to a museum? Whether she prefers early-morning or late-night sex?"

An image flashed through his head of Portia in his bed, her hair fanned across the pillow, her eyes still heavy with sleep but heavier still with desire, reaching beneath the sheet and wrapping her hand around him. His body reacted as if his fantasy were reality.

For the span of a second, he read a reciprocal heat and interest in her gray-green eyes. She blinked and glanced down at clipboard. "I suppose those would all be considered getting to know someone better." Despite her composure, her voice held a husky note.

Rourke knew a moment of dejection and elation. Elation that for one unguarded moment he'd glimpsed an answering heat, interest, awareness.

Dejection that that was all he'd have—a glimpse. And in some weird recess of him, elation that she possessed the honor to walk away from this thing that simmered between them, since she lived with Danny, the love of her life.

Rourke drew a deep breath to clear his head. She wanted him to name someone he wanted to know better, and it couldn't be her. He gave her what she needed. "I'd like to get to know Carlotta Zimmerman better. She seems interesting."

Carlotta was, according to her dossier, actively involved in several children's charities. She seemed the least idle of the idle rich women he could choose from.

Portia looked mildly surprised. "Carlotta? Okay."

"Why does that surprise you?" Nearby, a bee droned in the bower above him.

"She's probably not who I would've picked for you. She's not as…" Portia stumbled.

"As glamorous? As flamboyant?" Carlotta was the shortest and the heaviest of the group.

"Well, yes."

"Do you think I can't look beyond the surface of a woman?" He held her gaze. "Is it just me, or men in general you think so little of?"

"I'm sorry. I've offended you and I didn't mean to." She apologized but didn't answer his question, and the mystery of what made Portia Tomlinson tick merely intensified for him.

PORTIA WATCHED Rourke gallantly divide his time between the women at lunch. Except Lissa, who'd been sent packing, making more than a few choice comments as she flounced out. You could always tell the correct people had been eliminated when they bitched and moaned their way out the door. Nonetheless, Portia'd been surprised that Rourke had eliminated her so early in the show. Lissa's net worth was more than the others' and she was hands down the most beautiful, if you discounted personality and disposition. But apparently personality and disposition counted with O'Malley, which took him one step further from being the boy toy she'd pegged him as.

Portia had gone back to her room after her briefing with O'Malley this morning and doubled up on her vitamins. She was usually healthy as a horse but she had to be coming down with strep or mono or some unnamed malady because she'd definitely felt feverish when he'd run through his litany of questions. Then she'd felt queasy when he'd expressed his interest in getting to know Carlotta better. And following the realization that there was probably more to O'Malley than just a pretty face and hot body, she'd developed a headache. So, she'd rushed back to her room and popped another vitamin pack.

And now, watching him charm his companions, and undoubtedly the viewers when this segment aired, she felt queasy again.

She was definitely coming down with something.

ROURKE ROLLED his shoulders to dispel his tension. They'd scheduled a break between lunch and whatever ridiculous activity they'd set up for this afternoon, and he needed it. He was definitely out of sorts. Eleven women were hanging on to his every word and all he could do was watch Portia, bemused by the way she tilted her head to one side when she conferred with Lauchmann, or Jerry the sound guy or any number of other people with whom she interfaced.

He was crossing the dining room when Jacey motioned him over. "You up for a quick camera lesson?"

"Sounds good to me." It was at least a distraction.

Jacey walked him through the equipment basics and allowed him to pan the room and zoom in on several areas.

"This is so cool, I can see why you love it," he said handing her the camera, his mood definitely improved by the impromptu Camera 101. It was more interesting than a mere distraction.

She grinned. "There are worse ways to make a buck."

Rourke hadn't planned to, but he pulled a move straight from high school and went fishing for information on Portia. "Yeah, but it must make relationships tough, being gone for two weeks or more at a time. I know Portia's boyfriend called the first day we were here."

Jacey did a double take. "Highly unlikely. Portia doesn't do boyfriends."

What the hell? She'd mentioned a live-in.... Was Danny short for Danielle? "You mean she's...."

"A lesbian?" Jacey laughed, which was much more like a bark than an actual sound of amusement. "No, although one of the set designers has a serious crush on Portia and wishes that were the case. As far as I know, Portia doesn't date. She works her ass off and that's about it."

Then who the hell was Danny, the so-called love of her life?

Rourke knew he should drop it, but he seemed singularly incapable. "I thought she lived with a guy."

Jacey's look was as openly speculative as his question. "I don't know. She keeps to herself. I know she has a kid, David or Darrell or something like that."

He's the love of my life…I live with a geek.

"Danny?"

"Yeah, that's it, Danny. I grew up with a single mom who worked and it doesn't leave a whole lot of room or time for fun."

Everything clicked into place for him, and Rourke tried shrugging off his obviousness. "I was just curious about her. She doesn't talk much about herself."

Jacey's look said she had his number. "Mmm. That's an understatement. She gets along well with everyone and pretty much gets close to no one. She sorta reminds me of myself," Jacey said with a grin, "but she plays better with the other children."

Rourke laughed again, but the wheels inside his head had shifted into overdrive. Portia had deliberately misled him. Not just once, but twice.

And he'd be very interested in finding out why.

"Geeze, this is really hot. Any hotter and the water's gonna boil," Jacey muttered, steadily filming the afternoon session.

Portia, standing behind the camerawoman, couldn't agree more. O'Malley and the princesses had spent the last hour and a half cavorting in the Turkish bath while discreet waiters served drinks. Watching bikini-clad, semidrunk women crawling over O'Malley, spectacular in swim trunks, was more than working her nerves, extra vitamin pack or not. She closed her eyes, dropped her head and massaged her temples.

"Holy shit, we've got a catfight," Jacey said. "Hey Portia, are you watching this?"

Portia jerked her head up. Maggie, the socialite whose sex video had surfaced on the Internet, grabbed Carlotta Zimmerman by the hair and screamed, "You friggin' cow, that's where I was sittin'." Maggie slurred her words slightly, but there was nothing wrong with her grip.

Carlotta flailed, trying to get Maggie out of her hair. "Let go, you bitch." She made contact, the slap ringing out in the shocked quiet.

Oh. My. God.

"Whore." Maggie grabbed another handful and yanked again.

"Slut." Carlotta grabbed the front of Maggie's skimpy bikini top and yanked, pulling the top down, leaving Maggie bare-breasted.

Portia stood frozen to the spot.

Maggie lunged toward the other woman, screeching like a fishwife, "We'll show everybody who's a slut."

The censors would have a field day with this. So would the audience at home, filling in the blanks.

O'Malley pushed between the two women. "Easy, ladies." Maggie caught him with a right hook. He worked his jaw, but didn't take a restraining hand off either one of them, pointedly not looking at Maggie's free willies. "Ladies, I'd say this party's over."

Maggie climbed out of the water, stumbling along the way, pausing to pose for the camera. "This is my best side."

Maggie'd passed one too many drinks some time ago.

"Do you think she learned that at her Swiss finishing school?" Portia asked Jacey, coming out of shock mode.

"Oh, yeah. Daddy's dollars at work there." Jacey gave a raucous chuckle. "She could give lessons in the 'hood."

The rest of the women climbed out on the other side, surrounding Carlotta, giving the inebriated flasher a wide berth.

"Un-freaking-believable," Jacey said without taking the camera from her eye.

"Too bad we didn't know ahead of time, we could've filled the pool with pudding," Portia said. "Guess we'll be cutting back on the booze."

"Are you kidding? Our ratings just went off the chart. We just made reality TV history. And I don't think that was the booze at all. I think that was Maggie making sure she keeps a spot on the show."

"You're brilliant and so is she. That kind of stuff doesn't ruin the shoot, it makes it."

O'Malley hauled himself out of the pool, water sluicing down him.

"And that won't hurt our ratings either," Jacey said. "Okay, that's a wrap." She pulled the camera away and turned it off. "Burt's gonna have a freakin' kitten when he sees this." She nodded toward O'Malley toweling off at poolside. "Let's hope our beefcake doesn't come up with a bruise where she decked him."

For as many times as Portia'd referred to him as Boy Toy O'Malley and thought of him as just another pretty face, Jacey's "beefcake" struck her the wrong way. "He should ice it."

She left Jacey standing there and walked over to O'Malley. She felt absurdly prudish in her business suit when he wore only swim trunks and had just been treated to a free show of the best breasts Maggie's dad's money could buy. And his money had bought a big show. "Be sure you ice your jaw."

He shrugged his impossibly wide shoulders and a shiver slid down her spine. "She didn't hit me that hard."

"Better safe than sorry. We don't want to film you with a swollen jaw."

He shot her a look, an expression in his eyes that she couldn't define, but left her feeling flushed and unbalanced. "I'm going to my room to change. Why don't you bring me an ice pack," he said with a curious note of challenge. "I still don't have any plastic bags, but I do have quite a supply of—"

She cut him off. "I'll bring you an ice pack." She was irritable and probably on the verge of some terrible malady and she wasn't one of those simpering women in the Turkish bath. She wanted to tell him to fetch his own damn ice pack, but dutiful fetching topped her job description. Funny, she'd liked her job up until now. "Give me a couple of minutes."

She left him poolside and quickly made her way to the kitchen, where she rounded up a plastic bag and ice. Waylaid on her way out by a positively giddy Lauchmann, Portia was outside O'Malley's room half an hour later.

Her heart thumped wildly at the prospect of being alone with him in his room. Sans cameras. Maybe she'd worked in the business too long, but cameras kept people at arms' length, where she preferred them. She thought about Carlotta and Maggie.

She knocked on O'Malley's door. He yelled that it was unlocked and she let herself in. Locking his door was a good idea. He never knew when a drunk, naked, hostile woman might follow him. It could have just as easily been Maggie, with or without a bikini top, slipping into his room. Portia, however, held her counsel. He was a big boy and he could take care of himself. She might have to fetch his ice, but she wasn't his freaking mother.

He came out of the bathroom, fully dressed, but looking good enough to destabilize her knees. No. She most definitely wasn't his mother. Not even close.

She held up the bag. "Your ice."

He crossed the room and she was struck anew by how gracefully he moved for such a big man. He stopped in front of her and her world became O'Malley—his scent, the subtle rise and fall of his chest, the almost imperceptible sound of his breathing, the width of his shoulders, the blueness of his eyes, the curve of his mouth. Failed by her internal censor, she reached up and plied her fingers along his jaw. Warm, a faint brush of stubble. Her breath caught in her throat. "Does it hurt? Is it tender?"

O'Malley looked as mesmerized as she felt. "It's a little sore."

"Have you ever had two women fight over you before?"

"No." His voice was low and husky, his eyes dark. He tilted his head, leaning into her fingers still cupping his jaw. Oh, God, she was still touching him.

She meant to—really meant to—snatch her hand away, but he was such a beguiling combination of warm skin, rough seductive cologne, not to mention those lovely blue eyes that made her long for things she shouldn't...his taste, his touch.

She had no clue what they'd been talking about. The only thing she knew was that she wanted to kiss him more than she wanted to breathe. There was a list, longer than her arm, as to why she shouldn't, but she couldn't recall a single item on that list. Her urge to kiss him eclipsed everything else.

She slid her hand from his jaw to the back of his neck, her fingers curling into the texture of his thick, dark hair. His eyes darkened and he bracketed her waist with his hands. She pulled his head down to hers, until they breathed the same air. She stepped into him and...an icy cold penetrated her breast.

She jumped away from him, frozen sharply into reality, saved by the melting ice pack intended for her charge. She took another step back, totally appalled that she had almost kissed Rourke O'Malley.

Of all people, O'Malley. As if he wasn't assigned to her. As if she were one of the multitude of women flocking to the Website and chasing him down with panties in hand. At least she was still wearing her panties. Although she would've been pretty willing to peel out of them about two seconds ago.

She shoved the ice pack into his hand and took even a third step back, away from him, seeking sanity in distance. "You'd better ice that jaw."

He obligingly held the ice to his face, and with a distinctly predatory look, stepped toward her, closing the gap between them.

She looked at the heavy drapes lining the window, the brocade-covered chaise, the framed print on the wall of an intimate couple. Better the room's sensuality than losing herself in O'Malley. "That should help," she said, retreating farther.

"I'm already much better," he said, stepping forward.

They played a silent version of retreat and advance until Portia felt the press of the mattress against the back of her thighs and knew there was nowhere else to go. And it was happening again. Her heart pounded and she felt as if butterflies had taken flight in her stomach. A dark, hungry, sensuality stole through her.

"One question," he said, his eyes intense.

She swallowed. "Yes?"

"Why did you let me think Danny was a lover instead of your son? Are you involved with anyone?" O'Malley stood, ice pack to his jaw, his other hand by his side, but the heat in his eyes, the soft sexy timbre of his voice, touched her, wove around her, caught her up in the soft, hot folds of desire's blanket.

How did he know that? Of course any of the crew could've filled him in. Momentary panic assaulted her. She didn't want or need O'Malley interested enough in her to make inquiries. And the worst of it was, there was a smidgen of her, the woman in her that had responded to Sadie's teasing, that was flattered that he'd asked someone.

And *that* simply made her angry with both of them. She called on every ounce of her will to push away the want he aroused in her. His interest threatened her peace of mind and, given their respective roles in the show, was inappropriate. Who was she kidding? He'd asked her why she didn't like him, but she knew in a blinding moment of revelation that she'd been running from this overwhelming attraction since she'd met him.

"That's two questions, not one. You made an assumption I didn't correct. I prefer to keep my private life just that—private." She strove to keep her tone light, but cool and professional. Instead, her voice came out husky with a defensive note.

He tossed the ice pack onto the bed behind her,

but still, mercifully didn't touch her. "Your son is the love of your life, the geek in your life, waiting at home for you, isn't he?"

Okay, so she'd hidden behind Danny. She'd sensed his interest and deliberately let O'Malley misconstrue her situation because there was nothing safe or sane about O'Malley's interest and the feelings it aroused in her. "You said one question. I answered that."

"There's no man at home waiting to kiss every inch of you from head to toe until he's drunk from your taste, your scent and the sound of you moaning for him to stop or take you further? There's no one waiting to wrap his arms around you and hold you until you drift off to sleep afterward, is there?"

His words and low tone seduced her and her body responded to the fantasy he wove. Need blossomed inside her as surely as if O'Malley had greeted her at the door, stripped her naked and proceeded to make love to her with his sexy mouth. One of them had to stop this madness.

"Stop. Stop it right now." She looked away from the tender promise of pleasure and passion in his eyes. "What possible difference does it make to you? Why are you doing this?"

He touched her. One finger against her cheek, that drew her gaze back to his and flooded her with heat.

"Because you asked me if I ever broke the rules and I told you only if I wanted something desperately. And I do. You."

5

"WHY ME?" Portia looked like a cornered wild creature. A part of him felt guilty for pushing her so hard, but the part of him that recognized her reluctant response to him won out. "You have all those women, not just the eleven in the house, but all those women running amok after you. Why are we even having this conversation?" She raised her chin a notch, challenging him. He dropped his hand to his side and she stepped away so that she was no longer between him and the bed.

Why her? Why not any of the other women? Rourke shook his head. "Hell if I know. It really complicates things and I don't like things complicated. Maybe it's the way you move your head to one side when you're concentrating. Maybe it's the No Trespassing signs discreetly posted despite your friendliness with everyone. Maybe it's the sexy line from your ankle to the curve of your calf."

He scrubbed his hand along the nape of his neck. "I don't know, Portia. I wish I did because it's as if I'm on a damned roller coaster."

Portia's eyes widened but she didn't say anything.

"I feel this energy pulsing between us, I see something in your face, your eyes, and I think you must want me as much as I want you. I find out you don't have a lover, you have a son. But why let me think that? Because you're not attracted to me, but you can't tell me to back off? Because you are attracted to me and don't want to be? Hell, I don't know. I just know I'm frustrated with myself. All of those women, some of them very nice, all of them beautiful, and all I can do is feel your every movement, where you are in the room, what you're doing. Sometimes I even think I catch a whiff of your fragrance."

He didn't dare look at Portia. He didn't know what he'd see. Was she horrified? Embarrassed? And he couldn't seem to shut the hell up. "And I'm damn afraid that Jacey with her all-seeing camera is going to capture it on film so I can be humiliated by mooning over you in front of the whole damn world, or at least the parts able to receive a satellite signal. So, I suppose we're having this conversation because I lie in that bed at night and think about you beside me, beneath me, on top of me. Because I ache for just one kiss, for one moment to hold you in my arms, against me, to breathe your fragrance, your essence. To hear my name cross your lips. Not O'Malley, but my name." He turned to face her then, except she was studying her hands as if they held universal secrets, and he laughed in self-recrimination. "Through no fault of your own, you are driving me mad."

For a man of few words, he'd found far too many. No doubt about it—that qualified as a tirade.

Silence sat heavy in the room, his words settling into the space between them. She raised her head and looked at him. She was neither horrified nor embarrassed. Her beautiful gray-green eyes that usually hid so much hid nothing now. They reflected longing and a measure of despair that brought his heart into his throat.

"I've tried denying it. Disdaining you. Ignoring you. And still I'm attracted to you." Yes! He took a step toward her. She held up a hand to stay him. "And we shouldn't be having this conversation. Nothing can change. We each have a role to play here and this isn't it."

She still wasn't where he longed for her to be—in his arms. But her admission felt like a huge leap forward.

"You're right. But I want two things."

She was already shaking her head. "I don't know."

"Portia, please. I'm dying here. You wouldn't do two little things to save a dying man?"

The resolve etched on her face softened in the slight curve of her mouth. A glimmer of a smile hovered in her eyes. "I don't suppose you'll do us any good if you're dead. What are these two things that I can do to save you?"

"Say my name and one kiss." He spread his hands, palms up. "That's not so unreasonable is it?" Well, maybe it was. Exactly when had he, the most reasonable of men, passed the point of reason regarding Portia? When she'd touched him? When she'd helped him to his bed and unwrapped that condom? When he'd discovered she didn't have a man in her life so surely he stood a remote chance? When she'd seemed to forget herself and cupped his jaw? Was it all of the above or was it the first time he'd seen her on the set of *The Last Virgin* and everything had just been a slow spiral from there?

"That won't solve anything." Portia was much more reasonable than he was.

"No. It won't. But can it make things any worse?" Perhaps she thought she could look at him the same after one kiss. He knew better.

"Rourke." His name rolled off her tongue with a musical lilt, strumming through him, as if he were hearing his name for the first time ever.

She stepped closer. "I know this isn't a good idea." But she slid her arms around his neck, cradling his head in her hands. He wrapped his arms around her, content for the moment to absorb the touch of her hands against his skin and hair, the feel of her in his arms, her sweet scent. He sighed against her hair, savoring each moment, unwilling to rush touching her, tasting her.

"Rourke…" she breathed his name against his neck, her mouth warm and moist against his skin. He clamped down on the desire that gnawed at his belly like a hunger and cautioned himself to take it slow.

Framing her face in his hands, he bent his head and kissed her. At first it was a tentative exploration and then it shifted and changed. Everything deepened. Her tongue met his in an intimate dance of parry and thrust. Hunger replaced tenderness.

Reluctantly he pulled away from her. Breathing

had never been such an inconvenience. He was beginning to know Portia. She'd agreed to one kiss. He'd have one kiss and no more.

His chest heaving as if he'd just worked out, his breath still uneven, his body tight and hard, he rested his forehead against hers for a moment, reluctant to give up totally his proximity to her.

"Rourke…" He loved the way she spoke his name. Her face was flushed and her eyes were a soft smoky gray. Her lips were slightly swollen as if she'd just been thoroughly kissed, which she had, and he'd willingly sign on for duty again. This was yet another facet of the woman who so fascinated him.

She stepped away from him and he barely refrained from reaching to keep her. "You are so beautiful, you take my breath away."

She suddenly looked years younger. Flustered. Pleased. Unsure of herself. "You're too kind. It's more likely you just needed to come up for air."

Despite her flippant comment, she raised a hand to smooth her chignon into place and it was shaky. She'd been as affected by that kiss as he had. Her wristwatch alarm went off, shattering the intimacy between them, pulling them back into the reality of their respective roles. "You have to be at the salon in half an hour. But I need to talk to you first."

Rourke knew her well enough to recognize the transition. He also knew there wouldn't be another kiss or even a discussion of that kiss. Portia was back to business. "Go ahead."

"It's time for you to send another contestant

home but Lauchmann wants you to keep both Maggie and Carlotta on the show."

He ran his hand over his jaw, neither pleased nor surprised. "Let me hazard a wild guess—it's all about the ratings."

Portia nodded. "It is all about the ratings. That's why we're both here." She crossed to his bedroom door.

Granted, they were here for the show, but the chemistry between them…. "Wait," Rourke stopped her, unable to shake the notion that if she walked out the door without some resolution, they'd lose something invaluable.

Her hand on the knob, Portia pivoted to face him.

"What about us? Where do we go from here?"

"There is no us. There can't be any us." She squared her shoulders. "But if there was, the only place for us is nowhere."

"You're wrong, you know." He looked at her, unwavering. "I'll be there in half an hour, but you need to know every time I look at one of those women, every time I touch her, kiss her, I'm thinking of you."

She fled as if a demon from hell nipped at her heels. He knew because the same demon pursued him.

FOR THE past two days she'd watched O'Malley charm and flirt with his women and she didn't know if it was the power of his suggestion or chemistry or what but all that sexual energy seemed to be directed at her.

Portia wanted to do something she hadn't done in years…plop down and have a good cry. Or bang her head against the wall.

Neither seemed a particularly good option in the middle of afternoon shooting.

For years she'd kept her nose to the grindstone and all of her impulses in check. Now she had almost ten friggin' years of stored impulses exploding inside her, around her, and generally turning her busy but well-ordered life upside down. Yeah, she'd been coming down with something. A raging mother of a case of lust.

And there he was, the inspiration and object of her towering lust, surrounded by ten women all trying to put the make on them. And he wanted her. Cry or head-bang? She simply didn't know, and ignoring it didn't seem to be working.

And today was particularly unnerving. Lauchmann had changed up the day's schedule this morning. He was so pleased with the previous day's filming—according to him O'Malley was exuding a sexual energy that wouldn't quit—that he'd accelerated the schedule to shoot a scene originally planned for later. Today was the day she'd dreaded ever since she'd read the loose scene notes.

O'Malley wore sultan garb and each of the women, outfitted in belly-dance attire, would perform a dance for him and then present herself to him for a question. The salon drapes were drawn and muted lighting bathed the red walls in an intriguing mix of light and shadows. O'Malley sat on one of the low sofas like a potentate. Several incense candles burned, filling the air with exotic eastern scents. Evocative music flowed from a hidden sound system, a rhythmic mix of drums, tambourine and flute.

And damn him to hell, just before he'd entered the room, when she was checking with him on any last-minute questions, he'd reminded her that it was her he wanted performing for him in a harem outfit. Every look, every command, every touch would be for her.

When she'd read the setting notes, it had sounded like a scene straight out of B-movie. It didn't feel that way now. It felt sensual. She felt too aware of her own body. Aware of the swing of her skirt against her legs, the gentle cupping of her bra against her breasts, the insistent ache between her thighs. She was in a state of almost painful want, mired in arousal, which defied reason and logic.

"He's really blossomed on screen. He's gone from hot to really hot," Jacey said, without taking her eye from the camera.

Dear God, she hadn't in a moment of lustful insanity said anything aloud, had she? "Who?"

Jacey spared Portia a disdainful look. "Who do you think? Lauchmann? Of course, Rourke."

Was there a woman alive who didn't fall under his spell? At this point, she was ditching her pride and throwing herself in with the rest of the pathetic women of the world. "He's okay."

Jacey snorted. "Portia, you're either half dead or you're jacking me around."

"Come on, Jacey. Don't you find that get-up just a little over the top?"

A pair of loose, blousing pants rode low on Rourke's hips, an open vest only partially covering his bare, lightly furred chest and muscled belly with its dark V of hair that disappeared under the waistband. An amulet was artfully wrapped around his bicep. No one in wardrobe was going for authenticity. This was all about titillation. He should've looked ridiculous. Instead he displayed just the right hint of arrogance, command and humor that left her body tight and humming.

"You're kidding, right?" Jacey glanced up from adjusting her camera settings. "I plan to beg, borrow or steal that outfit before I go back to New York so Digg can play dress-up. And I think you're lying through your teeth. I think… "

Portia interrupted Jacey, sensing it was better not to know what Jacey thought. She capitulated with a defeated laugh. "Okay, he's really hot."

"He asked me about you," Jacey said.

Ah. He'd found out from Jacey. Not a big surprise. They were operating with a skeleton crew on the technical end. Wardrobe and makeup, however, they had out the wazoo.

"He mentioned Danny. I assumed he'd found out from someone on the set. It wasn't a big deal. He's just one of those people who's curious about other people."

"Uh-huh, and I believe in Santa Claus and the Easter Bunny. It didn't feel that way to me." Jacey shot her another look. They couldn't start filming soon enough to suit Portia. Then Jacey would have to focus on the camera and this conversation would be over. "He's a nice guy, beneath that pretty-boy face. Almost as nice as Digg."

Dammit, that was part of the problem. He *was* nice. And he seemed to have a brain. And personality. And integrity. And regardless of how friendly she and Jacey might get, Jacey was still the executive producer's daughter. The last thing Portia needed was Burt Mueller calling her on the carpet for impropriety. That would be rich, especially from someone with Mueller's past reputation for being a womanizer, on and off the set.

"Yeah. He's handsome, hot and nice to boot. And I'm sure he won't have any problem picking out an equally beautiful, hot, nice woman," Portia added, as much for her own benefit as for Jacey's.

Jacey spared her a sly look. "Oh, I have a feeling he's already found her. I can spot chemistry a mile away. Rourke was hot on the last set, but from the beginning I felt the real sparks were between Zach and Andrea."

Portia tried leading her down another path. "Maggie certainly causes some sparks."

"Hmmph. You and I both know Lauchmann made him keep her in the game so she can threaten someone else into another catfight and drive his ratings off the chart." Once again, Jacey glanced away from the camera and Portia felt pinned by the younger woman's laser gaze. "Ya know, there's one good reason we have rules—so we can break 'em. Digg and I met on a set."

Portia nodded in acknowledgment. "I heard."

"I can tell you heard I got fired for about a day. And no, I didn't get rehired because my old man's in charge. I got rehired because I'm good at what I do and the director was a turd. From what I've seen, you're a workaholic. You could use a little TLC," Jacey said.

Portia couldn't just walk away from the conversation. They should've been shooting by now. She desperately wished Jerry would fix his sound problems so they could get on with the filming.

"If I thought I did, work would be the wrong place to look for that," Portia said.

"Considering the hours we put in, work's about the only option," Jacey said with a disgusted snort. "You'll be shocked to know I'm a rule breaker from way back. I'm throwing out a wild guess that you aren't. There are times you have to break rules and do it with an attitude. But, unless you're trying to make a statement, the key to breaking the rules and getting away with it is discretion."

Portia was saved from answering by Jerry giving the thumbs-up on the boom mike. "Got it. Let's get this party started."

Carlotta entered the salon through the double doors, her hips keeping time to the music. She swayed and swirled across the room and around Rourke on the divan. She was a decent dancer and Portia knew a moment of stabbing jealousy at Rourke's lazy, sexy smile. And as if he were tuned into her thoughts, he chose that moment to look at her. It may have looked as if he were glancing toward the camera, but his look rocked through her. *Every look, every touch is for you.*

Carlotta ended her dance, bowing at his feet. The music lowered to a background level and O'Malley posed the question he'd been told to ask in a silky, commanding voice that sent shivers down Portia's spine, "If you had me for a night, what would you do?"

"We'd go out to dinner and then maybe some shopping before we went back to your place."

What? Pathetic. If Portia had a man like O'Malley at her disposal for the evening she'd spend her time *shopping?* Carlotta Zimmerman was an idiot with a capital *I.*

"And would we shop for something *interesting?*"

The way Rourke caressed the last word immediately brought to mind naughty lingerie and massage oils.

"Shoes. I really like shoes. I have a closet built especially for my shoes."

Make that a double idiot. Beside her, Jacey bit back a snort of laughter. Rourke, looking somewhat surprised by her answer, seemed hard-pressed not to laugh as well.

Portia wouldn't spend her time shopping for shoes if she had him for a night. Unfortunately, she'd spent far too much of her time, both waking and sleeping, imagining what she'd do with, to and for O'Malley.

Tara Mitchells came in next. She was tall and willowy but not nearly the dancer Carlotta had been. Portia's mind wandered.

So, why not just go ahead and have a little fling with Rourke O'Malley? Maybe because she had to work with him. Why not just wait until after the shooting and then if they were still interested in one another.... No way. That implied something more long-term, more than a fling and she wasn't about to go there. She knew other single moms whose main focus was to get married or remarried. No thanks. She'd done all right by herself and Danny so far. She didn't have any interest in dating. Not only did she lack the time, she also wasn't willing to open Danny up to a barrage of men coming and going in their lives.

Particularly now when Danny was hungry for a male role model. It was evident in the way he'd glommed on to his grandfather, Portia's dad. But dating didn't mean marriage and she couldn't see herself ever getting to the marriage stage. Marriage meant trusting, opening yourself up to betrayal.

She'd learned the hard way to rely only on herself. People made mistakes and you could cut them slack for that. They weren't necessarily stupid. But when they didn't learn from their mistakes and repeated them, then they qualified as stupid. And Portia was a lot of things, but she certainly didn't want to be considered stupid.

However, this *was* her last location assignment. Rourke O'Malley lived on the other side of the continent. She was southwest, he was northeast. She'd fought it, denied it, all to no avail. He did something for her. In a big way. He was doing something major for her now. Portia had no idea how the whole room didn't know that she'd like to push the other women aside and claim him herself.

The dancing lasted an interminable amount of time. Or at least it seemed that way to Portia. Not that O'Malley seemed to mind all the gyrating and hip-thrusting coming his way.

Finally, Maggie was the last woman to dance. She stepped onto the back of the divan, bracing one foot on the side and one foot on the back, her crotch poised over his head.

A few of the women gasped, one giggled—probably Carlotta the idiot. The entire thing irritated Portia beyond measure. Maggie shook her tasseled breasts and undulated in time to the music, leaping off the divan as the song ended. She leaned forward, her breasts on either side of Rourke's neck.

"You had a question for me, Master?" she said.

With a wicked grin, he looked up, rather than left or right, which would have put his mouth right next to her breasts, and asked her the same thing he'd asked the other women.

"I'd pretend I was a genie in a lamp and if you rubbed me just right I'd make three wishes come true," Maggie practically purred.

Portia longed for the detachment she'd mentioned to O'Malley. She longed for the woman who didn't stand around, practically aquiver with lust during a shoot. She knew what she'd do if she had Rourke O'Malley for a night. She'd get him out of her system.

Perhaps Jacey was right, there was something to be said for discretion. Tonight, one way or another, there'd be a woman in O'Malley's bed. And she planned to be that woman. If she could beat Maggie there.

ROURKE ROLLED his head on his shoulders. Geeze, he was wound tight. He had a newfound respect for actors. Not that he was Tom Cruise by any stretch of the imagination, but on this "reality" show he was definitely an actor. Lauchmann, the producer, had told Rourke how pleased he was with the shoot so far. He'd reminded Rourke of the proverbial cartoon character with dollar signs in his eyes. According to Lauchmann, Rourke "sizzled" on the screen. Luckily, Lauchmann was clueless that all Rourke's sizzle came from his intense attraction to Portia that seemed to grow exponentially every day. Or hell, maybe Lauchmann knew and was willing to look the other way because he was getting what he needed for his show. Nothing in the inside workings of TV production, particularly "reality" TV could surprise him anymore.

He pulled a bottled water out of the minifridge in his room and took a long, quenching drink, but that didn't cool him down. His heat was internal. Sexual. It was going to take more than water to quell the fire inside him. A knock sounded on his door and he almost groaned aloud. Please, let it be anyone other than Portia. He was so wound up he didn't think he could take one of her debriefings tonight, where he looked but couldn't touch. Where she was near, yet separated by an emotional distance he couldn't seem to span with her.

He crossed the room to unlock the door. Let it be Lauchmann, or one of the wardrobe ladies here to pick up the pants and vest he was still wearing, or one of the maids with towels, or any of the other crew or staff. Hell, at this point, Maggie tracking him down would be preferable to another no-touch close encounter of the Portia kind. With any luck, it wouldn't be her.

He flung open his door. Luck had taken a holiday. Portia, wearing a khaki-green suit that brought out the green in her eyes, stood there clutching her clipboard. Rourke wondered briefly if she even slept with the damn thing.

A wave of desire slammed him. Maybe it was the outfit, maybe it was all the pent-up desire, but he felt reckless, dangerous and he let her see that in his eyes.

"May I come in?" she asked with an underlying breathlessness. There was something different about her tonight. Maybe edginess was catching.

He knew his smile had a sharpness to it when he stood to the side and swept his arm out in invitation. "What can I do for you this evening, Ms. Tomlinson?" In a perfect world, what she'd like for him to do for her would coincide with what he very much wanted to do for her. But luck had skipped town and it wasn't a perfect world.

"Wardrobe is shorthanded tonight. Cindy Lu is sick. So I offered to help out and pick up your costume," she said looking down at her clipboard, as if consulting a note there.

"Well, give me a minute and I'll get the costume

to you and then you can cross me off your list for the evening."

"I thought I could help you with that," she murmured, seemingly fascinated by something on her clipboard.

Okay, he'd misconstrued a situation with her once before and he wasn't about to set himself up again. "How's that?"

"I could help you out of that costume, Rourke," she said, looking up. What he saw took his breath. Naked desire that echoed his own burned in her eyes. This was no cool, shuttered glance, no calm dismissal, no retreat behind a closed door. This was need and passion and all thought fled his methodical, reasoning brain except the singular idea that she wanted him as much as he wanted her and she wasn't presenting a litany of arguments but rather was saying his name in that low, husky tone that nearly brought him to his knees.

"Portia." He reached for her and then pulled back. "If I touch you, I'm not sure I'll be able to stop."

She walked toward him, spanning the gap that separated them. "Maybe I don't want you to." She trailed one finger down his naked chest and he shuddered.

It was his turn to be surprised. "What?"

"I said I want you to touch me and I think I'd prefer if you didn't stop once you start."

He almost asked if she was sure. He almost asked how this would work tomorrow. He almost asked how long she could stay. But instead, he realized none of that mattered. Whatever she was willing to give, he'd take, and, he hoped give even more in return.

"Let me make sure I've got this right. You're offering to undress me and I get to touch you and not stop?"

"That pretty much sums up the situation."

He started to pull her into his arms, but she was holding onto that damned clipboard of hers like a lifeline. "Give me that."

She handed it over and he tossed it onto the coffee table. "I hate that thing."

"My clipboard?" she asked with a laugh as he pulled her hard against him.

"You hide behind it like it's a warrior's shield."

"Maybe I do."

He found the three pins holding her hair in place and pulled them out, dropping them to the floor. Like a shimmering silver-blond curtain, her hair fell past her shoulders. He immersed his hands in the silky mass and buried his face against the fine texture, breathing in her clean, fresh scent. He was definitely a dork at heart. He'd wanted her, and only her, for weeks, and now he had her in his arms and didn't know what to do. He stood, his face buried in her hair, paralyzed by his own want.

"You're exquisite. Fragile," he said.

She leaned back in his arms and looked up at him. "I'll take exquisite, any woman would. But there's nothing fragile or breakable about me. I'm tough."

He traced his finger down her delicate jawline, her throat's slender column, traversing her collarbones and beneath her suit edge to the soft swell of her left breast. Her heartbeat raced beneath his fingertip. "What about your heart?"

She shook her head, her hair skimming the back of his hand. "Especially not my heart. That's not even a remote option. So don't worry about my heart." A hint of melancholy marked her smile. Her professed invulnerability rendered her all the more vulnerable. "But you can carry on with exquisite all day," she said, pressing the swell of her breast against his fingertips.

Rourke didn't know exactly what or who had driven her to lock her heart away so securely. He suspected Danny's father. And he'd find out why later.

Right now, he was going with what he did know. And at that moment, Rourke knew exactly what to do. He knew exactly what Portia needed. She needed to be loved. And he knew just the man for the job.

6

PORTIA DIDN'T NEED Rourke to worry about her heart, although it was rather sweet and unlike the men she knew. She needed him to put to bed, lay to rest—every other bad pun she could think of—this restless longing, this incredible ache he'd awakened.

For ten years she'd gotten by nicely without wanting a man. Sex with Mark had been okay, a bit of a disappointment, so abstinence hadn't been such a hardship. She'd been her own island and after all that time, damn it, Rourke came along and made her want and need as she never had before. It stood to reason, if he was the cause, he was also the cure. She'd get this behind her and she'd be good for another ten, maybe even fifteen years.

For a brief second she considered the risk to his heart but then dismissed the notion. From her life observations, men didn't lay their hearts on the line with sex as so many women were prone to do. As she'd done once before. But she'd learned from her mistake.

Portia had waited so long, her hands shook with need as she laced them behind his neck and pulled his mouth down to hers. She greeted him with a hot, openmouthed kiss. All that pent-up sexual energy had her in a flux. She felt as if she couldn't wait another second. But then again, she wanted it to last. She wanted to take it slow, let it go on and on; after all she was saving up for another long haul.

She closed her eyes and lost herself in the sheer joy of their kiss. The taste of his mouth, his heat, the sweet mating of his tongue with hers, the faint rasp of his beard against her skin, his scent, his strength tempered by gentleness.

He raised his head. "I've wanted you since I first saw you on the set of *The Last Virgin*." That left her as breathless as his kiss. "I didn't want to want you." He laughed ruefully. "But sometimes free will doesn't stand a chance." Rourke shifted, raining hungry kisses along her jaw, down her neck, his hands spanning her lower back, pulling her closer, tighter against the length of him. "I didn't stand a chance, once I'd met you."

She, who kept everyone, except her immediate family at arms' length, especially men, felt an intimacy in his touch, a desire for closeness that was alien yet didn't send her running for the door.

Portia pressed closer, reveling in the feel of his body against hers. It was as if his chest had been made for the press of her breasts. "I didn't want to be attracted to you either." She slid her hands beneath his vest, caressing his naked back. "Not even a little bit. You weren't part of my plan." Slick, wet desire pooled between her thighs where the hard ridge of his arousal pressed intimately. Her entire body shuddered at the sensual contact she'd fore-gone for so long. Actually, she hadn't foregone *this*, because *it* had never been like *this*. "I've fought the good fight, but sometimes surrender isn't giving up."

"I still can't quite believe you're here." Rourke dropped to the loveseat and pulled her down onto his lap, molding his fingers to the curve of her shoulders. "You are so beautiful."

"Hmm. I bet you say that to all the girls," she teased, but a very real part of her needed his reassurance that this was about her. Especially after he'd spent the evening being entertained by par-tially clad women performing exotic dances.

His blue eyes, like a cloudless sky on a hot sum-mer day, were intense. "There've been far fewer *girls* than you seem to think. And it's not a line. It's the truth. You take my breath. Make me ache."

Given the women he'd been bombarded with, his words were even more meaningful. And with the way his hands and his eyes caressed her, she felt beautiful. And sexy and suddenly young and more carefree than she had since…perhaps ever. "Well, then…thank you."

He brushed his thumb over her cheek. "I've never met a woman like you, Portia. You're spe-cial."

God, it should have sounded like a bad line out of a bad script, but the way he said it and the way he touched her, made it poignant. She'd felt special with Mark, Danny's dad. She'd believed that he'd wanted her because she was who she was. But then after she'd wound up pregnant and he'd been so quick to skip out, she'd figured out that it wasn't her at all, but that she'd been vulnerable and available and that Mark had used her. That had been apparent enough when he'd moved on so quickly to the next available, non-knocked-up girl.

But with Rourke, she truly felt special. He had his pick of women and there was something about her, Portia, that floated his boat. He wanted her because she was Portia Tomlinson. And even though she wasn't going for a relationship, it was a nice feeling. *She* did it for him. And, heaven help her, he certainly did it for her.

"I've never met a man like you, either. You're one of a kind," she said.

It wasn't just the fact that he was gorgeous, it was the total package. The way he talked to a person as if they were the only one in the room. His slightly old-fashioned gallantry and courtesy. And beneath that handsome, polished exterior, she saw his geekiness. Weird as it might be to some people, it was even more of a turn-on to her. It made him real. Not so much like getting naked with Michelangelo's *David* or some other model of male perfection.

"I don't even care if you say that to the other men in your life," he said, a light reference to her earlier comment.

"No, Rourke. Only you."

As if her answer gave him immense satisfaction, he dipped his head and breathed a sigh against the base of her throat, his breath warm against her skin.

He nuzzled a series of kisses along her collarbone until he met her suit jacket.

He hesitated, his eyes questioning her, letting her set the pace.

She sat back from the hard wall of his chest. "This is in the way," she said, unbuttoning her jacket.

His eyes burning brightly, he slid the jacket over her shoulders. His fingers trailed a line of fire along her bare skin and down her arms. He briefly closed his eyes and then reopened them. "I want to remember you like this. Beautiful, disheveled, sexy."

Her heart hammered in her chest. "You are the most gorgeous man I've ever seen," she said, leaning forward to press her lips to his bare chest. He was big and broad and well-muscled. Heat flash-pointed through her when she tasted the texture of his skin.

She flicked her tongue against him, finding his flat male nipple. His heart hammered beneath her questing tongue and he groaned her name against the top of her head. He reached around her back, searching for her bra hook.

With a wicked smile—at least she hoped it was wicked and sultry because that's how she felt—she reached between them and unsnapped her bra. "Front hook."

"Once a geek, always a geek," he said with the sexiest smile she'd ever seen.

Still holding her bra together, although it was unhooked, she teased him, "I told you I have a soft spot for geeks. And a hot spot. And something of a wet spot."

She saw a flicker of surprise in his eyes, quickly followed by heat at her sexy playfulness. She'd sort of surprised herself, but hey, she'd made the decision to be here and she wanted to experience it to the fullest.

Despite her bravado, she knew a moment of uncertainty. Her breasts weren't as pert as they'd been at seventeen, the last time she'd been naked in front of a man. As if he were tuned into every nuance of her, Rourke gentled his hands over hers and opened her bra, revealing her.

He didn't say anything. He didn't have to. The look in his eyes said everything. She shrugged out of the bra, the cool air and his hot gaze sliding over her bare skin. Rourke traced his fingers across the slopes. His touch felt wonderful and her nipples peaked in anticipation. She dropped her head back and leaned back, bracing herself on her hands, offering herself to him. He rolled her turgid points between his fingers and the sensation coursed through her, notching up the intensity of the throb centered between her thighs. Instinctively she writhed against the erection pressed against her buttocks and the hands on her breasts. He bent forward and traced a delicate path around her areola with his tongue.

"Yes," she panted. But it wasn't enough. He licked a similar pattern on her twin peak and she arched toward him.

"Tell me what you want. Do you want me to stop? Do you want more?"

She was on fire. She'd never wanted anything as badly in her life as she wanted him to take her in his mouth and assuage the torment.

"Yes. More. Harder." She wasn't capable of saying more than that.

His mouth, warm and wet, closed over the aching crest and she cried out.

It was intensely erotic to be dressed from the waist down and naked above.

He slid his hand beneath her skirt and touched her through the damp satin of her panties. The first tremor of an orgasm shook her. Rourke pushed aside the cloth barrier and his fingers swept her slick swollen fold and the nub beyond, his hard-on tormenting her from behind. His mouth crushed against hers, his tongue mimicking the movements of his fingers and Portia gave herself over to the orgasm that rocked her.

ROURKE, his fingers still slick from her, smoothed his hand over her belly, awed he was here, making love to this incredible woman, and that for the time being he could touch her so intimately, yet so casually.

She looked up at him, her hair spilling over the edge of the sofa, her breasts with their darker tips bared, a satisfied smile curving her lush mouth, her delicious bottom pressing against his erection. All of a sudden Rourke understood why men beat on their chests, why they fought wars over a woman's touch.

"If this was an old movie script, I'd carry you to my bed and finish having my wicked way with you. Ravish you. Isn't that the way it goes? The sultan doesn't want the available harem girls? Instead he wants the fair foreigner," his voice dropped, "and the sultan always takes what he wants."

"I think you've got it right so far." Her voice was low and throaty, her eyes not nearly so slumberous. There was a different kind of glint in them now. He'd definitely turned her on.

"Hmm. And once he has his way with her, she becomes his willing love slave." He ran his finger along the seam of her lips and she took his finger into her mouth, sucking it, laving it with her tongue. The sensation arrowed straight to his throbbing penis and he surged against her buttocks. He withdrew his finger and trailed it down her throat and her chest. "Opening her tender self to his every whim." He caught her nipple between his thumb and forefinger and she ground against his shaft. He continued his journey down her body. "His every desire." He palmed her mound through the layers of skirt and panties.

Panting, her eyes alight with sensuality, devilment and challenge, she sat up and straddled him, her skirt riding up to the tops of her thighs, her sex just out of reach of his erection. "I think that script goes another way." She leaned forward until her nipples teased against his chest, trapping his shaft between her and his belly. "The sultan becomes enslaved by the very woman he sought to conquer." She slowly slid up his cock and he nearly came at the contact, despite the layers of clothing between them.

He dropped his head to the sofa back and caught her hips in his hands, sliding her along the length of him again. And again.

He shuddered, suddenly unable to take any more of her sweet torture. He grabbed her beneath the buttocks, slid her up the rest of his body and stood with her half tossed over his shoulder, her breasts against his back, her woman's fragrance tantalizingly close to his face. He covered the distance to the bed in three strides, ripped the covers back, and tossed her onto the bed. "We'll just have to improvise when we get to that part."

He stood at the edge of the bed, looking at her sprawled against the beige silk sheets. Still watching her, he opened the bedside table drawer and tossed an entire box of condoms on the bed. Not looking away, Portia slowly unzipped her skirt and slid it, along with her panties, down her hips, her legs and dropped them at his feet. She opened the box of condoms, pulled out a foil packet, and opened it. She lay back on the sheets, spreading her legs, giving him the glimpse of paradise he was so hungry for, and wet her lips with the tip of her pink tongue. "Do you prefer Master or Master Rourke?"

That drove him straight over the edge. He dropped the foil square on the bed, shrugged out of the vest and pulled off the pants. She offered him the package and he quickly sheathed himself. Wrapping his hands around her thighs, he dragged her to the edge of the bed and she spread her legs wider to accommodate him.

He could barely think beyond how much he wanted to be inside her. "Portia, I don't want to rush you…I want to make sure you're ready…"

A look crossed her face he didn't understand. As if she were enjoying a private joke. "Rushed? Not at all. I'm definitely ready."

He nudged into her and stopped, savoring the sensation of her tight wet heat gripping him. Portia gasped.

"Are you okay?" he asked.

"Oh, my....yes." She wrapped her legs around his hips, urging him forward with her feet against his buttocks.

It would be so easy to thrust into her, but Rourke kept it slow, easing into her until she was panting and his hands shook. And then it was out of his control because she bowed up, taking him as far into her body as she could, her muscles clenching around him, gripping him.

"Portia…" She felt so good.

"Rourke…"

They performed the intricate steps to the dance as old as man, the music inside them growing wilder, faster. Portia writhed beneath him like a woman possessed. Rourke held on to his self-control until she cried out with the first wave of her orgasm and then he came with her.

Rourke collapsed beside her, rolling her on her side to face him, still inside her, reluctant to break their connection. She lay very still, her eyes closed.

"Portia?"

She opened her eyes to a lazy half-mast. A sated smile curved her lips. "I've never felt this good before in my life. Now *that* was perfect."

"We *are* pretty incredible together," he said, pulsing deep within her.

Like a curtain-fall at the end of a play signaling to the audience that the suspension of belief was over, her expression changed as reality replaced their lovemaking. She carefully disentangled herself from him, slipped off the side of the bed, and disappeared into the bathroom.

Within a few short minutes, she came back into the room, and gathered her clothes off the floor. He'd hoped she would stay a little longer. A lot longer.

She picked her panties and skirt up from beside the bed. "Don't go," he said.

She paused and looked at him through the sheer material at the corner of the bed. "I have to."

"Not yet." His blood felt thick and hot and it was already starting to pool in his sex again just seeing her naked through the gauzy material.

"I've already stayed longer than I should have." There was a hint of wistfulness and melancholy about her smile. "Have you forgotten that a camera recorded when I came in here? We've already spent too much time *talking*."

She pulled on her panties and slipped on her bra.

"Oh, hell. I did forget."

She zipped up her skirt. "Neither one of us can afford to forget. It's why we're both here." Shrugged into her jacket and buttoned it.

He wanted to say to hell with why they were both here. He wanted to pull her back into his bed and sleep with her by his side through the night. He wanted to wake up with her head on the pillow next to his, her soft body curled into his, and make love to her all over again until she shattered around him again. He gave in to the temptation.

"And what if we said to hell with why we're here?"

"You know neither one of us can do that. You've got a contract and I...well, my stakes are high, too."

"What are your stakes?"

She finger-combed her hair and neatly twisted it behind her head, securing it into place. "It's not just my job. If this goes well, I get promoted to a studio position and that means I'm home with my son."

With each zipper, button, hairpin she became inaccessible once again. It was like unwrapping a Christmas present only to have it taken away and put on a closet shelf where you could see it but couldn't play with it.

Rourke plummeted from the euphoria of great lovemaking to the other end of the spectrum as he considered the weight of their respective obligations. Her son was counting on her and Nick was counting on him.

Dammit. He'd find a way to make it all work. He had to. She was worth it. "When can I see you again?"

She didn't pretend to misunderstand. She shook her head. "I don't know. I should say this isn't going to happen again...."

"No," he said.

She smiled at his vehemence. "But I don't think that's realistic. You know you have to spend some time with one of your candidates when you're not with them as a group." She picked up that damn clipboard and slipped her feet into her shoes.

Once again, she was so calm, cool and collected and Rourke was frustrated with the situation he'd gotten himself into. Damn it all if he didn't feel like some high-priced man-whore. She could at least pretend that the idea bothered her.

"Doesn't it bother you to know I'll be with another woman?"

She jerked her head up at that. "How can you ask me that? You think I won't go out of my mind thinking of you touching one of them the way you touched me? Do you honestly think I want them to know how you taste? How you feel? Do I want to think about one of them wearing your scent on her skin the way I am?"

Remorse flooded him. "I'm sorry. I'm just frustrated…." He ran his hand through his hair.

"I know. I've got to go." She knelt on the edge of the bed and pressed a hard kiss to his lips. "I'll see you tomorrow morning at nine."

She started to walk away and then turned around, scooping the pants, vest and shoes off the floor by the bed. "Almost forgot these."

He watched his amazing woman walk to the door. His. Definitely his.

"Portia…"

She turned to face him. "Yes?"

"I'm not usually a jerk."

She smiled, her skin flushed, "I didn't think you were."

No. He wasn't usually a jerk, but then again, he'd never been in love before.

PORTIA CLOSED her bedroom door and leaned against it. She'd run into both Lauchmann and Jerry the sound guy on her way back to her room. Amazingly enough she'd managed to carry on an intelligent conversation about tomorrow's schedule without either one of them looking at her any differently than they usually did.

Amazing since she felt as if her whole person screamed *sex*. She felt like sex, from the tenderness between her thighs to the hypersensitivity of her breasts. She smelled like sex. God knows, she still tasted Rourke against her tongue.

She had never, ever suspected sex could be that good. A ten-year hiatus after Mark hadn't been a hardship. But sex with Rourke had been a whole new experience, opened a whole new world to her. Or maybe it was just this first time. Like the first drink of water to a woman who was parched or the first glimmer of spring after a cold winter.

Still leaning against the door, she kicked off her shoes and pulled the pins from her hair. It tumbled past her shoulders and she closed her eyes, picturing the look on his face when he'd taken her hair down. She sighed. She could still feel his fingers in her hair, his breath against her skin.

A knock on her door shattered the moment. Perhaps because she was caught up in him, her first thought was Rourke. He shouldn't come to her room. She opened the door. Jacey stood on the other side. Relieved he hadn't been that insane, and unreasonably disappointed in equal measure, Portia pasted on a smile. "Hi."

"Can I come in?" Jacey asked.

Gathering her wits, Portia stood aside. "Of course. Come in." She closed the door behind the other woman. "Have a seat," she offered her the ladderback chair tucked in the corner.

"Nah, that's okay." Jacey scrutinized Portia. Maybe it was the discerning eye of seeing things through a lens. Perhaps it was that she looked for details instead of the whole picture. Maybe it was because women were generally more discerning than men that she saw what Lauchmann and Jerry had missed. Regardless, Portia knew the instant that Jacey realized she'd just been tumbled by Rourke O'Malley.

"Oh." A slow smile joined the knowing glimmer in Jacey's eyes. "You'll definitely be interested in this. I thought you needed to know we're having some camera troubles."

Portia reached for her clipboard. "What kind of camera troubles?"

"Specifically with the camera in Rourke's wing of the building. Seems we're having a problem with it recording between nine at night and seven in the morning. It seems to be looping back on itself," Jacey said.

Great. Like they needed this. "When did you first notice?"

"Today."

"So it didn't record last night?"

"No. There wasn't a problem last night."

Portia looked up from her clipboard. "Well, if you just found it today, how do you know it won't work until tomorrow morning?" This wasn't making any sense.

"Because sometimes the totally unexpected happens and short-circuits the wiring we've worked on so carefully." She offered a typical Jacey shrug. "Shit happens. We may not have that camera working properly before we're through. And of course if someone," she looked pointedly at Portia, "were entering or leaving O'Malley's room between those times, it wouldn't be caught on tape."

Click! The proverbial lightbulb went off in her sex-saturated brain. Jacey had fritzed the camera so Portia and Rourke could have time together. She *was* the original rule-breaker. "Why are you telling me this, Jacey?" Portia asked, wondering silently just what Jacey's true motivation was.

Jacey offered her signature shrug, but a look in her eye indicated she knew *exactly* what it was that Portia really wanted to know. "Because you're the associate producer and I thought you should know. Because rules are meant to be broken. Because some opportunities come once in a lifetime." She shifted from one black-booted foot to another. "And I'll have to seriously consider offing you if this ever goes any further 'cause it's so damn stinkin' Pollyannaish, but because everyone deserves to be happy."

Great. Jacey had morphed into a Goth matchmaker and Portia found it incredibly touching that the tough young woman would do this.

"Thank you for telling me. I'll schedule things accordingly. That's good information to have," Portia said. Message sent, received, acknowledged and it was time to change the subject. "Speaking of happy, how's Digg?"

"Lonely," Jacey said with a cheeky grin. "But other than that, he's good."

And Jacey was obviously no fool. She knew Portia had said and heard all she wanted/needed to hear. She opened the door and stepped into the hall. "He's calling me in ten minutes. I'll tell him you asked."

Jacey left and something almost as warm as Rourke's lovemaking embraced Portia. Friendship. She'd discovered a lover in Rourke and a friend in Jacey. It had been a strange—no, that wasn't really right—a magical night. She picked Rourke's costume up from the chair where she'd tossed it and rubbed her cheek against the soft material. It still bore his scent. She breathed deeply. Tomorrow would be soon enough to get it back to wardrobe. Tonight she would pillow her head on his clothes and drift off to sleep with his scent beneath her.

THE FOLLOWING MORNING, Portia hurried along to the study they'd set up as a temporary production office. She and Lauchmann met each morning before her daily meetings with Rourke.

She was late. She was never late. But she'd slept like the dead last night and overslept this morning.

She calmed herself with a deep breath before entering the study. She hated being late.

Instead of being annoyed at her tardiness, Lauchmann looked like the cat with a canary. "O'Malley's bagged someone and I want to know who she is," Lauchmann announced without preamble.

Portia sank into the seat on the other side of the round table. Holy hell. How did Lauchmann know O'Malley had, as he so poetically put it, "bagged" someone? Portia glanced down at her clipboard, taking a moment to carefully school her face into pleasant impassivity. She looked back up at Lauchmann. "What makes you think he's sleeping with one of them already?"

"Empty rubber wrappers." Lauchmann winked at her. "Try saying that six times fast."

"And you know this how?"

"I slipped the maids a couple of bucks to let me know if they found any. There was one the other day—" *ice pack* "—and one this morning." *The real McCoy.* "The man works fast. But I don't have to tell you, this is just the kind of thing enquiring minds, as in our viewers, will want to know. So, it's your job to find out which one of our lovelies has succumbed to stud-boy's charms."

He'd paid the maids to snoop through Rourke's trash? She really, really didn't like Lauchmann. He was a decent producer, but the same couldn't be said for his status as a human being.

Portia crossed her legs and leaned back in her chair, striving for casual and confident. "I don't think he's going to tell. That was one of the things the viewers liked about him so much on the *The Last Virgin*. He's a gentleman with ethics."

Lauchmann peered at her suspiciously and nausea rose. Dear God, if Lauchmann the Crude ever had so much as an inkling....

Portia shrugged and continued quickly, praying Lauchmann was easily distracted. "That's the feedback we got from the Websites." That and orgasm-waiting-to-happen fame. Sister, that woman didn't know the half of it.

He nodded, crossing his hands behind his head and leaning back in his chair.

"If he won't tell, it's your job to find out, P.T." She hated it when Lauchmann called her P.T. "If there's anything women like more than a nice guy, it's a bad boy. They'll eat up an ethical gentleman who's a stud beneath it all. Find out from the women. Ten women, well, nine after today, all chasing the same guy. Whoever's in the sack with him probably can't wait to let the rest of them know she's snagged him this far." He waved his hand in the air. "Don't you women have some kind of intuition thing for that crap?"

Portia resisted a near-hysterical urge to raise her own hand and confess to being bagged, snagged and the culprit in the empty-rubber-wrapper escapade. For once, it might render the ever-disgusting Lauchmann silent.

But the satisfaction wasn't worth her job.

No, it was now her job to try and come up with another woman in Rourke's bed.

7

"WOULD YOU like to take a wild guess what my big assignment is today?" Portia asked.

Rourke crossed his arms over his chest to keep from reaching for her. What he wouldn't give for five minutes of uninterrupted privacy so he could greet her the way he wanted to, with a thorough kiss. What the hell? Why not go for broke? A proper good morning would include losing their clothes and discovering one another.

Ah, but he was supposed to be guessing today's mission. He knew what he wished her assignment was. "Let's see, you're supposed to make sure my every need is met and you're here to pick up that list."

It felt good to flirt with her even if he knew he shouldn't. He wanted to position himself in front of the camera and announce to the world at large that she was his and he was going to do his damnedest to make her think of him as hers.

Portia twirled her pen between two fingers. "Better than that."

They didn't exactly have the privacy he craved, but no one else was around. He looked at her, letting her see just how much he wanted her again. "Honey, it couldn't get any better than that."

Aside from an answering flicker of heat in her eyes, she ignored his comment. "Lauchmann informed me you've bagged someone. He knows because he paid the maids to snoop through your garbage. They narked on the condom wrappers."

"You're kidding. No, you're not kidding. He's going through my garbage?" Rourke wasn't sure whether he was more amused or annoyed.

"Not personally. But, yes, he's having your garbage sifted through." Portia rubbed her hand over her forehead as if warding off an impending headache. "I should have thought about the garbage."

All his good humor evaporated. This felt sordid. No way in hell Portia knew that was going on, but he hated she was even involved with a company that ran such a seedy show. "Have you ever considered a career change? You have too much integrity for this," Rourke said.

Her head snapped around. "Most of the time I really like my job, and for the most part it doesn't compromise my integrity," Portia said. "And speaking of integrity, *you* are the one who signed up for this show, not me. When they pay you the kind of money they're paying you to be here, I suppose they figure they own your garbage as well."

He'd pissed her off. He ran a hand over his hair, silently counting to ten, because, damn it, her jibe had hit home. Increasingly, he felt like a high-rent gigolo.

"Did he give you any indication he suspected us?"

"Thank God, no. I doubt I'd be here now."

He thought she was overreacting—Hollywood wasn't exactly puritanical in its outlook. "I can't imagine sleeping with me would ruin your career. I'm sure it's not the first time it's happened."

She recoiled as if he'd struck her, and he realized how his words had sounded.

"Not you, honey. I didn't mean it's happened with you before. I meant the industry in general."

"It does. It's not terribly professional, however."

"Portia, I trust you, and I want you to know you can trust me. I would never do anything to hurt you."

She looked at him without comment, obviously unable to tell him what he needed to hear, that she trusted him. "Lauchmann is going to breath down my neck unmercifully until I give him a name."

"The studio may have bought my garbage, but they don't own me. I've kissed those women, but I'm not going to sleep with any of them. Not to cover you with Lauchmann or for ratings or—" he almost said "or to keep Nick out of prison," but he caught himself in time "—for any other reason. I'll just have to store the wrappers in my suitcase."

"That won't work. I wouldn't put it past him to have the maids count the condoms in your bedside table, just to make sure."

"Are you telling me that I've got this huge supply of condoms and I can't use them with the woman I want to?"

"Lauchmann's antennae are up. So, as long as I'm that woman, no."

"Don't worry about this, Portia. I'll figure something out. I'll take care of it. And yes, you're the only woman I'm interested in using them with. And I can't wait until tonight to convince you."

BEING WITH Rourke was like being a sponge on the edge of a puddle of water. Once she started soaking him up, it seemed impossible to stop. She knew that the puddle wouldn't be there forever. But while it was, she'd become patently incapable of ignoring it.

Tonight it was late, nearly midnight as she made her way through the mansion.

Rourke was waiting for her inside his room.

"Did you enjoy today? It looked as if it was a good time," Portia said by way of greeting, anticipation making her babble.

He locked the door behind her and effectively trapped her against it with his big body. The increasingly familiar heat and warmth and sexual desire shook her.

"I'm having a good time, now," he said in a low, sexy voice. He leaned down and slowly, deliberately, thoroughly made love to her mouth, suckling her lower lip, exploring the tender recesses with his tongue and then upping the pace, his tongue plunging inside, leaving her aching, wanting him between her thighs.

Rourke tugged her blouse free of her skirt and touched her belly and her ribs, and then his big hands were cupping her breasts, kneading, massaging her. He took her nipples between his fingers and lightly plucked and tweaked until she moaned into his open mouth. She arched her throbbing mound against the rigid line of his erection and he ground against her. He tugged harder at her nipples and she felt as if her body were on fire. She reached between their bodies and cupped him, stroking him.

God, she was discovering a whole sensuality and sexuality she'd never known she possessed. And now she was making up for it in spades. Driving her wild. It was as if he got off on destroying her composure. And he could. And he did. And he was a nice guy, both inside and out. And he was a geek. And he was so hot it made her hot.

He'd asked her about fantasies before. And somewhere along the line, throughout the years she'd managed not to think, not to fantasize. But now, since Rourke, she found herself prey to fantasies. She didn't want to think too much about why he'd awakened her fantasies, she only knew he had. And tonight she'd share one and make him wild. She wanted to see the light of reason leave his eyes.

She broke their kiss and pushed him away. "Will you do something for me?"

He didn't hesitate or question. "Yes. Anything."

"I want us to do something for one another."

Apparently that was the right thing to say. His smile was nothing short of wicked and the heat in his blue eyes scorched her. "Tell me more."

"There are rules," she said, her excitement heightened by simply giving voice to her fantasy.

She trailed a finger down his chest, past his belly to his belt and felt his muscles contract beneath her fingertip.

"Your rules?"

"Yes."

"And what happens if I break a rule?" He crossed his arms over his chest.

"Then you don't get to play my game."

"I'm all ears."

She glanced pointedly at his hard-on straining against the front of this slacks. "That's not the way I see it."

He laughed, grabbing for her. She danced away.

"Rule number one. No touching each other."

"Is this a game or some subtle form of torture?"

"Maybe both." She walked toward the bed, glancing back at him over her shoulder. "Do you want to play?"

"If it's with you, I definitely want to play. So, rule number one is no touching. What's rule number two?"

"Rule number two is we take our clothes off."

"I definitely like two better than one," he said, laughing. "Okay, okay. How many more rules are there?"

"Only one. You have to do what I tell you to."

He raised a brow, but he was definitely intrigued. And turned on. "Let the games begin."

She swept the coverlet and the sheet back and sank back onto the mattress. "Undress for me." She leaned back on her elbows. "And do it like you mean it."

"I think being in charge of all those people every day has gone to your head."

She scooted to the mattress edge, her skirt riding up her thighs. "Should I take my toys and go home?"

"Oh, not yet, baby. You and your toys—" his gaze lingered between her nearly exposed thighs "—stay right where you are."

Rourke unbuttoned his shirt and made a production of sliding it off his broad shoulders, flexing his pecs, then slid it down his arms. He tried to shuck it off and it was stuck at the wrists. "I forgot to unbutton the cuffs."

Portia laughed as he worked the buttons free. He was so achingly handsome and sexy and dorky all at the same time.

Laughing along with her, he finally freed himself of his shirt. "Dammit woman, I'll give you something to laugh about." He turned his back to her and did that goofy thing everyone had done at some point in time in junior high when they wrapped their arms around themselves and ran their fingers up and down their sides, as if they were making out with someone.

Portia fell back on the bed, laughing. It was the weirdest sensation to laugh so hard in the middle of being so sexually tense. He turned around, grinning.

The grin faded, to be replaced by a carnal, predatory look. He crossed the room to stand in front of her. She was still sitting on the bed so that put his crotch pretty much at eye level. He reached for his belt and the muscles in his belly rippled and her mouth went dry. She wasn't laughing now. He unbuckled his belt and let it hang. Portia swallowed.

Rourke bent down, his movements slow and deliberate, until his head was between her thighs. Her muscles clenched and she grew slicker, hotter. His nostrils flared, as if he were a wild animal picking up her scent. A dark, wicked smile curled his lips and coiled through her. He braced one hand, big and masculine with its smattering of dark hair, on the bed next to her, oh so close to her thigh, but not touching her. He slid off one shoe and sock and then shifted his weight to repeat it on the other foot. As he straightened, his forehead, nose and chin nearly skimmed her crotch. She could almost feel his warm breath, his heat against her bare thighs and panties. He'd only taken off his shirt, shoes and socks and she was nearly panting.

He dispensed with the button on his pants and then he slid the zipper down, the sound mingling with her raspy breathing. He hooked his thumbs in the waistband and pulled his pants down, moving forward to step out of them, putting his jutting erection, hard abs, and muscular thighs closer. Tantalizingly, temptingly close. His harsh breathing rang in her ears. The smell of him bordered on dizzying— the aroma of male arousal, masculine skin and aftershave.

He pivoted and turned away from her. In one movement, he took off his briefs and she faced the back side of a spectacular specimen of manhood. Broad, muscled shoulders, sculpted back, a perfectly firm, tight ass, and muscular legs. She reached out to run her hand over his well-formed buttocks, jerking her hand back at the last second, remembering her no-touch rule.

"Tur—" her voice was a rusty squeak. She swallowed and tried again. "Turn around, Rourke. Please," she tacked on softly.

He did as she asked and faced her, legs braced, a big, dark, hard man. All humor and perhaps a fine veneer of civility were gone. She might be giving the orders, but she wasn't altogether sure any more that she was in charge. Once again, this time without even touching her, he'd driven her crazy. It was exhilarating and frightening to ride the edge of such intense sexual desire. She wanted to do the same to him, for him.

She looked at his erection and rimmed her tongue around her lips. His cock, sleek and hard, pulsed, reacting as surely as if she'd touched the tip of her tongue to him. He drew a harsh breath but still didn't speak.

She slid off the bed and moved to the foot. "Lie on the bed and I'll undress for you. Would you like that?"

"Very much." She watched, appreciating the ripple of muscles and the sheen of his skin as he stretched out on the sheets.

Portia knew a moment of hesitation. It was much easier to watch than to be watched. But wasn't this part of her whole fantasy, being watched, being wanted for who she was?

She deliberately left her hair up. She knew

enough after this week that Rourke liked it down.
She'd save it for later. He'd propped himself against
the plump pillows on the bed. The bed post and silk
drapings cast his face in shadows. She couldn't see
his eyes, but she felt the heat of his look searing
every inch of her as she bared herself to him until
the only thing she was left wearing were her
pumps. She left the pumps on because she'd seen
more than once how he'd watched her legs and because they made her feel sexy, and right now she
was feeling very, very sexy. She raised her hands to
her head, aware that it lifted her breasts like an offering, and pulled the pins from her hair. His groan
echoed from the bed. Undressing for him left her
very wet, very aroused.

"Spread your legs," she said.

"Oh, honey," he murmured as he widened the V
of his legs. She climbed onto the bed and crawled
across the mattress until she was between his thighs,
close enough to feel his heat, but still not touching.
Bracing her hands on either side of his head she
leaned forward, poised over him, her breasts just out
of reach of his chest, his erection nearly nudging her
mound.

His warm breath gusted against her face. "What
do you think of my game so far?" she asked, her
lips close to his ear.

"I'm not sure if I'm going to die of anticipation
or of pleasure."

"*La petite mort.*"

"What now?"

She sat up, away from him and slipped back a

bit, but still between his legs, on her knees, her legs apart, the air cool against her slick heat. "Now, you sit back and watch. And if you like what you see, tell me. And if you don't, well you can tell me what you'd like to see."

She lightly ran her hands up her thighs, pausing to stroke her belly, and then cupped her breasts. Portia repeated his earlier actions, squeezing and kneading them, plumping them for his benefit. And hers. He fisted his hands in the sheets. "Play with your nipples." His voice was nearly guttural.

She rolled her nipples between her thumbs and forefingers and the sensation went straight to her womb, arcing her back with pleasure. "Like this?"

"Yes. Tell me how good it feels."

"It feels almost as good as your hands on me." She brought her fingers to her mouth, wetting them, and then brushed her wet fingers over her sensitive tips. "And that feels almost as good as your mouth on me."

"Sweet…oh…Portia."

She skimmed her hands over her belly and along her thighs. "Should I touch myself?"

"Yes."

She ran one finger lightly along her aroused slickness. "I am so wet. Doing this for you makes me so hot. Do you wish you could touch me?"

"Yes."

"I could touch me for you. Would you like me to do that for you?"

"Yes."

She slipped a finger along her wet cleft and

moaned at the intensity of the touch, of the situation. "If you want me to do that again, you need to do something for me."

"Anything."

"I would really like to touch you. I'd like to stroke you, taste you. But I can't because we have rules we can't break. So will you touch yourself for me?"

He wrapped his fingers around his shaft and she touched herself. She slid two fingers into herself and clenched her muscles, tightening around them. "This gets me off. I'm so tight and I know this is how it feels to you."

"Oh, baby, you don't know how good it feels when I'm buried deep inside you. And you can't possibly know how hot it makes me to watch you do that."

Aching, raging with a need so desperate she thought she might cry, she added a third finger and worked it in and out of herself in a rhythm that he followed. She found her nub with her other hand and waited until Rourke gasped her name and saw his body go rigid that she relinquished the last vestige of sanity and they climaxed together.

ROURKE CAME OUT of the bathroom after cleaning himself up. Portia lay sprawled across the bed, still naked, obviously exhausted because she was asleep. He'd like nothing better than to crawl into bed with her, wrap her in his arms and spend the night together, but that was a recipe for disaster.

He sat on the edge of the bed. He'd wake her up.

In a minute. Or two. Or five. He studied her in repose. He could look at her a lifetime and never tire of her, from the exotic slant of her eyes—inherited from her Malaysian grandmother as he'd learned this week—to the classic line of her nose, the flat planes of her cheekbones, the fullness of her lips and the slight pointiness of her chin.

Good God, she'd been on fire tonight. She'd set him on fire. While it wasn't the same as actually making love to her, it had been intensely erotic. He wasn't quite sure when he'd ever been so almost unbearably aroused. And coming from a woman of such immense reserve and composure, it had been all the more titillating.

Unbidden, he wondered how many times she'd played that game before and with whom. There was still so much of her that was a mystery to him.

He had no idea whether her son looked like her. How did she feel about Danny's father? Had she played her game with him? Did she still play with him? Stranger things happened than exes sleeping together. Where did she want to be in ten years? Was there room in her life for him? And he desperately wanted there to be room in her life for him.

He could make it through the next week or so. He could play the reality TV game to keep Nick out of prison and make sure Portia kept her job. He could feign interest in Carlotta. God knows he'd pretended not to care about being the brunt of jokes often enough. He had that down pat.

It was the aftermath that scared the hell out of him. He wasn't Einstein, but he knew that Portia planned a "have a nice life and good-bye" when this was all over. The catch was, he thought there was a very real possibility that the nice life he craved was with her. While he didn't make enough to bail Nick's ass out of hot water—Nick had "borrowed" a serious amount of moola—he made decent money. Enough so that Portia didn't have to waste herself on mindless shows like this.

How'd he feel about a ready-made family? He didn't know squat about kids, but he did know all about being a geek. He knew from life experience that a geek was a geek was a geek whether said geek was ten, fifteen, twenty-five or thirty. So, he and Danny already had something in common. And they both loved Portia, yet another thing in common.

Rourke felt much less amenable about an ex-husband, but he'd take the bad with the good. Portia being the good, the ex being the bad. And he was jumping way ahead of his game. He had his work cut out for him, convincing her a "them" existed beyond this shoot.

He stretched out beside her and gentled his hand over her shoulder. He loved the soft, satin feel of her skin. Bending, he pressed a light kiss to her lips. "Hey, Sleeping Beauty, wake up."

She blinked her eyes open and offered him a sweet, lazy smile that made his heart sing. "Hey, you."

Then it was as if reality hit and she jackknifed up on his bed. "Oh, my God, what time is it? I didn't spend the night did I?"

He gentled her back down onto the mattress. "Relax. You were only asleep for about ten minutes."

Amazingly, she did relax, curling up next to him. "What did you think of my game?"

He smoothed his hand across her hip. "I think I'd always like to be on your team." He propped himself on one arm. "Portia…" He brushed a lazy kiss across her nose.

"Umm?" She pressed a sweet kiss to his chin.

He smoothed her hair from her shoulder. "Tell me about Danny."

She didn't move, but she withdrew as surely as if she'd rolled away from him. "Danny's off-limits."

A physical slap would have hurt less. He'd just shared mutual masturbation with this woman and she still didn't feel as if she could discuss her son with him? But he couldn't force her to trust him, confide in him. All he could do was respect her decision. But he could still ask other questions. "What about your ex? Danny's father?"

"What about him?"

"Does Danny stay with him when you're on location?"

"He's not my ex. We were never married. I got pregnant and he got MIA." Her cold smile broke his heart. He could only imagine what it had done to hers. "Danny's dad's a crackhead. He wasn't when we were together. Responsibility's not exactly Mark's strong suit. He came by once when Danny was a baby. Not to see the baby—he's never been interested in Danny. He wanted money to score a hit. We haven't seen him since."

It was too goddamned easy to read between the lines. Rourke, not a violent man, wanted to tear the bastard limb from limb. Small wonder that his baby had built Fort Knox around her heart.

"How old were you?"

"Seventeen. I wasn't wild and I didn't sleep around. Mark was my first." Her expression was defiant. As if he might judge her and find her lacking.

"And the bastard just left you to have and take care of a baby by yourself when you were seventeen?"

"Pretty much." There was so much more that she wasn't saying, he could see it in the shadows in her eyes, but he didn't ask. He was almost sorry he'd brought it up. He didn't want to bring her pain, even remembered pain, but it explained so much about her. "I'm extremely lucky that I have a great family. My parents were disappointed but understanding. They've been great. They kept him while I worked and went to night school and still I've felt guilty because we were a financial strain. I don't know what women without family support systems do. And my younger sister Mellina's been great as well. Danny's very much adored by his aunt and grandparents. In fact, they dote on him. And the feeling's mutual."

That he could relate to. His family was close as well. It sounded as if they shared similar backgrounds and he wanted her to know that. "My parents would do the same, and it would be a financial strain on them as well." He really hadn't planned to, but he suddenly found himself confiding in her about Nick.

"So, you didn't come on the last show or this show because you were interested in finding the woman of your dreams?"

"No." He smiled ruefully. "I'm a quiet, homebody kind of guy. I'd have opted for a much less public format. I'm not a player."

She smoothed her fingertips across his chest. "You gave up your privacy to bail your brother out and protect your parents. You're a good man, Rourke O'Malley." The tenderness in her eyes wrapped around his heart and embarrassed him all at the same time.

"You would do the same for your sister if she needed you, wouldn't you?" He knew the answer before he asked the question.

"Absolutely. Tell me more about your family," she said.

Yes! She wanted to know about his family, about him. He *wasn't* just a warm body in her bed. He gave her the abbreviated version of the O'Malleys. She was so easy to talk to. He could spend the rest of his life talking to her…among other things.

"However, they don't have any grandchildren, much to their dismay. They're just waiting for the day. For some reason they don't consider my dog a worthy stand-in for a grandchild," he said.

She laughed. "Dogs are nice but no, they aren't grandchildren. And there are no grandchildren because…?"

Was she indirectly asking him why he wasn't

married? "Because it's up to me and my brother Nick. Nick can't seem to settle on one woman and me, well, I've just been very content with Watson, my miniature schnauzer who thinks he's a person, and my own company."

"Danny wants a dog. They're not allowed in our apartment building," she said. "I've been saving for a downpayment. When I get this promotion, we should be able to afford a condo or maybe even a really small house and I've promised him a dog. A small dog. He doesn't like big dogs, they're intimidating to short, skinny kids."

Asking her outright had gotten him the cold shoulder but she was telling him a whole lot about her son just in general conversation. And he loved it. "Then you ought to look into a mini-schnauzer. Unless he just wanted a puppy, you could even look at a rescue group. I got Watson when his previous owner died. They're great city dogs. But they're smart and need exercise. Of course, if you have a smart kid with lots of energy, that could work out to be a love match. And they're good watchdogs. Very protective of the ones they love. A dog can be great company for a nerd. Dogs don't care how geeky you are or whether you walk around in your socks and underwear."

Portia laughed. "Okay, okay. I'm sold. You've convinced me. You sound like Danny. He'll have to send you a thank-you letter for lobbying his position."

Her laughter died, as if she just realized what she'd said, implied. That they'd be in touch afterward. That Danny was no longer off-limits.

She sat up, the curve of her naked back a study in feminine grace and beauty. "I need to go. It's late and we both need some sleep."

She gathered her clothes and disappeared into the bathroom, returning once again cool and remote in her suit, her hair gathered in a smooth chignon.

But this felt different, because he knew the passionate woman beneath the cool exterior. And she was beginning to know the real him.

8

"So, who's in the sack with O'Malley?" Lauchmann asked from behind his desk.

Great. After hours of enduring Rourke being fed—*fed* for God's sake—by the contestants, now she had to put up with Lauchmann grilling her. "I didn't make a lot of headway."

"Well, why the hell not?"

"They have busy schedules and I can hardly walk in and demand to know which one's sleeping with him."

Even Lauchmann seemed to recognize the rationale of that. "I suppose. Dammit, there's got to be a way to find out. The hall camera isn't showing anything. He didn't get any action last night, no condoms in the garbage, so he will tonight. Especially after the food fest with them feeding him with their hands and rubbing up against him." Lauchmann's eyes glittered with the excitement of a voyeur.

Oy. He was maxing out her ick factor. "I'll talk to the ladies again."

"Forget that. I've got a better idea. We're not seeing anyone on the video feed in the hall so they must be coming in through his window."

"Through his window?" Portia almost giggled at the thought of her climbing through Rourke's window. Not that sex with Rourke wasn't worth it. Her temperature went up several degrees just thinking about it. And then lying in his bed afterward, talking about their families. She'd never known anything like that. It had been wonderful and frightening, because she could get used to it. "You think one of our pampered princesses is climbing through his window?"

Lauchmann narrowed his slightly bulging eyes, which gave him a totally weird look. "Yeah, I do. And you're gonna find out who. I want you to hide in the bushes outside his window tonight and then when she goes in, you go get Jacey and her third eye and the two of you wait in the bushes for her to come back out." He literally rubbed his hands together.

She couldn't help herself. She laughed. "You're kidding."

"You know, P.T., promotions and pay raises go to employees who go that extra mile when a job needs to be done. It'll be great footage and we'll rule the ratings."

Sure. Why not? She could say she had. It wasn't as if she was actually going to catch anyone and then she was a team player. "I want this show to be successful as much as you do. I'll stake out—" she couldn't even bring herself to say hide in the bushes "—his window tonight after I've briefed on tomorrow's shoot."

"I knew I could count on you. Maybe there's

more than one of them. Now, that would be *really* hot."

Portia didn't even want to go there with Lauchmann. "I'd better go then. I don't want one or more of his women to slip past me."

ROURKE STRETCHED, his body wound tight. He'd thought filming would never end tonight. They'd had the nine remaining contestants each prepare a dish for him and serve it to him for dinner. He supposed it was meant to be funny because he couldn't fathom that any of them had ever made herself toast. He'd played the game, but it had seemed to go on forever.

Aside from the time they'd had together this morning on the terrace, he hadn't managed another moment alone with Portia all day. And he was aching for her. He needed her. Needed to hold her close, bury his face in her hair, feel her heart beat next to his.

A knock sounded on his door. Anticipation coursed through him as he crossed the room. Finally. He opened the door. Shit. Maggie stood in the hall.

She slipped past him, into his room, without waiting for an invitation. Double shit. "Come in," he said with dry sarcasm as he closed the door.

"I wanted to talk to you privately without cameras and microphones. Your room's not bugged is it?" Maggie plopped onto the couch and patted the spot next to her in invitation.

"No. My bedroom's not wired," he said, ignoring the spot next to her and standing instead. He had to admit he was damn curious as to why she'd sought him out for a "private" conversation. He'd discovered in business that often the best tactic was silence. Most people couldn't stand silence and would speak to fill it. It often garnered more information than asking questions.

Maggie crossed her legs. "You're probably wondering why I'm here."

"The thought had crossed my mind," he said.

She smiled at his dry tone. He had to give Maggie credit. It would've been totally lost on Carlotta.

"I thought maybe we could cut a deal," she said.

She had his attention. Rourke dealt in business deals all day, every day at work. He recognized when someone shifted into negotiation mode. This wasn't personal, this was business. "I'm listening."

"Do you know that whoever you pick gets her own TV show?" *That took care of the twist.* She took one look at his face and smirked. "I can see you didn't. I knew none of those ninnies would have enough sense to cut a deal. They're all hoping to win on chemistry." She rolled her eyes and shook her head.

"Here's the deal. You've got plenty of chemistry, but I don't think it's with any of us."

Maggie was truly a surprising woman. There was more going on with her than he'd ever suspected. Actually, he hadn't thought about Maggie. He hadn't really thought about any of them because Portia'd had him locked up tight from day one. "Okay," he said, neither confirming nor denying.

"So, I want to discuss what it'll take to get you to pick me. I want that show. If it's sex, I don't have a problem with that." She rose, walked up to him, wrapped her arms around his neck and kissed him, her tongue seeking entry while she rubbed her large breasts against his chest. Rourke simply felt mild amusement that she thought he'd find that sexy. He stepped back and firmly held her at arm's length.

She wet her lips. "I don't even mind if you want to make a little home movie."

He shook his head no and she slanted him an arch look. "I think you've got the sex covered. If it's money, name your price."

Rourke put the length of the couch between them. He didn't need any more surprise attacks. "The network's paying me plenty. Why should I pick you?"

"Because I'm no more interested in a love match than you are, tall, dark, and handsome. And all the others, while they want a TV show too, want you along with the show. They want you to want them. I'm the only one who isn't going to cause a stink when we conveniently discover we're incompatible after all."

"How do I know this isn't some studio setup?" he asked. They had dug through his garbage, after all.

"I guess you don't."

"If you want this show so bad, why don't you just have your father buy it?"

"My father's bought my whole life." She smiled.

"And I know what you're thinking, 'Spoiled little rich bitch, what a tough life.' Do you have any clue how invalidating it is when your whole life is bought and paid for? I want to earn this on my own. Plus, Daddy will just be mortified to have his daughter with her own tawdry TV show."

She was looking for personal validation through a reality TV show? And she was willing to earn it on her back or buy it with her father's money. Not to mention she was looking to bite the hand that fed her. Hell, he'd bet money Maggie'd leaked that home video that had circulated on the Internet to humiliate dear old dad. Rourke thought she should spend some of her megabucks on a good couch—in a therapist's office. "You know you could always do charity work in some third-world nation."

"That would wreck my manicure." Her smile was deprecating. "So, what's your price for naming me the lucky lady to win your heart?"

At the end of the show, he had to pick someone. And she could get Lauchmann off Portia's back. "You act as if you've seduced me and then when it's all over we go our separate ways and no one's ever the wiser."

"That's all? Didn't you hear me say I'd pay you? I'd willingly screw you." She eyed him up and down like a female wolverine. "It wouldn't be a hardship."

Not even if hell froze over. This chick was nuts. "Not necessary. Just convince everyone else you did."

Like timing straight out of a Greek tragedy a

knock sounded on his bedroom door. Portia? What the hell, he wasn't laying any odds. "Excuse me a minute," he said and turned his back to Maggie who had a hand to her chest. He crossed the room and opened the door.

"Hi," Portia said, a lustful smile lighting her eyes and curving her mouth. "Can I come in?" she asked and then peered past him, her smile fading.

"Uh…I was just finishing up—"

Maggie wrapped her arms around him from behind, her hands linked dangerously close to his equipment. "What do we have to do to find a little privacy, darling?" She slid around him, still clinging, ducking beneath his arm. "Oh, hi," she said to Portia, "we were almost in the middle of something." Rourke glanced at Maggie. Her blouse hung open, her hair a mess, her lipstick smeared. "You know, the middle when you get to the juicy part."

He'd just told Maggie to convince everyone they were lovers and she was obviously sealing the deal with an impromptu performance. *No*, his mind screamed. *Everyone but Portia.* But he could hardly say it since that would tell Maggie everything she needed to know. And that kind of information would definitely be dangerous in Maggie's twisted hands.

"Could you come back later?" he asked Portia.

That calm cool that he'd grown to dislike so much because it hid the woman beneath, returned. She offered them both a smile. "That's not necessary. It was nothing that can't wait until tomorrow. I'm sorry I interrupted. Enjoy."

She turned on her heel and walked away, soon disappearing around a corner.

Maggie was still wrapped around him, rubbing herself against him almost unconsciously. "The offer still stands, you know. We might as well finish this the old-fashioned way. The middle is *very* juicy."

It would leave him rock-hard in about two seconds flat if it was Portia saying that and doing that. But it wasn't. And why the hell couldn't this woman take no for an answer?

He reached for her, but it was to button her blouse. "Maggie, you're a unique woman," yeah, she was nuts, "but I think we'd both regret it if this went any farther. You deserve your own show because you think fast on your feet and that was very convincing." Her clothes were intact and he wanted her out of here. He ushered her out the door. "You can be sure I'll hold up my end. Thank you."

She preened, pausing in the hallway. "It seemed like a good opportunity to get the ball rolling. I guess that means we've got a deal."

Yeah, they had a deal and he had a mess.

FOOL. FOOL. FOOL. Portia's footsteps seemed to echo the word along the hall. She knew better than to trust a man. Especially a man who looked as good as O'Malley. Especially a man put in his position. He needed money and he was being pursued by wealthy women. And she'd known there was no exclusivity between her and O'Malley.

No, her outrage was that he'd chosen Maggie, of

all people. Maggie who he'd ostensibly wanted to send packing. Brash, crass, lots of money and no class, sleazy Maggie with the juicy middle.

She wanted a shower. A nice hot, long shower. That was what she needed to wash her hands of O'Malley. He was only another bit player in this lousy show and tomorrow was just another day of filming and thank God she only had another six days on this miserable location. And if there was a silver lining here, it was that she could now tell Lauchmann with certainty that O'Malley had "bagged" Maggie Duchanne.

And why did she care? It wasn't as if she and O'Malley were any part of anything that remotely resembled a commitment. As she'd told him that first day in his room, he could sleep with all the contestants, all at the same time if that's what he wanted and he possessed the stamina.

Who was she kidding? She wouldn't have been any happier to find Carlotta or Tara or any other seminaked woman in his room. She was angry with herself for believing him when he told her she was special. For being gullible after so many years of being careful.

Before she made it back to her room, her pager went off. O'Malley. He'd certainly made quick work of finishing up with Maggie. The part of her that had just found her lover in his room with a half-dressed harlot wanted to ignore the page. The part of her that was paid to be on call 24/7 for the show's star couldn't.

She unlocked her door and toyed with the idea

of turning her pager off, but years of conditioning wouldn't allow her such a personal indulgence. Instead, she picked up the phone and dialed his extension. "What can I do for you, Mr. O'Malley?" Not even the slightest quiver marred her cool, professional, even tone. She even managed to inject a friendly note.

"I need to see you. We need to talk."

"Can't this wait until morning, Mr. O'Malley? It's been a long day and surely we can go over any details you need to cover at tomorrow morning's briefing." Her voice was cool and rational, unlike his brusque tone.

"Surely it can't wait, Ms. Tomlinson." He mimicked her formality. "If you're too exhausted to make the trip to my room, I have no problem coming to yours. *But we will talk tonight.*"

You'd think he was the injured party. Of course, the best defense was a good offense.

"I'll be there in a few minutes, Mr. O'Malley." She shot the phone a bird. *Take that, Mr. O'Malley, and put it where the sun don't shine.*

"I'll be eagerly awaiting your arrival, Ms. Tomlinson."

She left her room, barely refraining from slamming the door, and marched back through the labyrinthine turns to O'Malley's room. For the second time that night, she knocked.

Almost immediately, he flung the door open.

She peered around the doorframe. "Is it okay to come in? I don't want to interrupt another tryst," she said politely, her tone downright solicitous. "Or did you have a break between appointments and thought you might squeeze me in?"

He took her arm and pulled her inside the room, slamming the door behind her. In a second, she found herself pinned to the wall, his arms on either side of her.

"It was not the way it looked," he said before he swooped down and branded her with a kiss that staked his claim.

She loathed herself that his kiss could stir her to instant arousal even though she knew he'd just kissed another woman without benefit of a camera. All her calm, all of her control was swept away by a landslide of anger and passion.

She wrenched her mouth away and wrapped her arms around his neck, fisting her hands in his hair. "I know what I saw," she said and before he could answer she ground her mouth against his, her tongue battling with his.

Rourke broke the kiss. "A little trust would go a long way," he said, unbuttoning her suit jacket. He bent and suckled her breast through her blouse and bra and the sensation pierced the veil of anger surrounding her.

"What should I think?" She dug her nails into his shoulder as the exquisite sensation of his mouth fueled a passion born of ire and betrayal.

He lifted his head and kissed the column of her neck while he cupped her buttocks in his hands and pulled her hips against him. "Maybe you should think that I was cutting a deal to give you the story you needed for Lauchmann."

She pulled his shirt over his head and threw it to the floor. "It looked like a win-win deal for the two of you." She swirled her tongue over his nipple and heard his sharp intake of breath. She, who was usually so even-tempered and level-headed, was blinded by anger, desire and white-hot jealousy. She wanted to punish both of them. Him for betraying her and her for allowing it to matter.

He unzipped her skirt and pushed it down past her hips. He delved beneath her panties and wrapped his hands around her cheeks, squeezing and pulling them apart and her sex ached for him. "She came to me," he said, his breath ragged, his erection pushing against her belly.

Her fingers didn't fumble as she worked free his belt and unzipped his pants. "That's no surprise. Women can't resist you, O'Malley." Her laughter echoed her bitterness. "*I* can't resist you, even knowing I'm second in line tonight."

He pressed his forehead to hers. "Damn it, Portia, I don't know how to convince you. She wanted to cut a deal so that I would pick her and she'd wind up with the prize show. She offered me both sex and money."

She stroked his erection through his underwear and he shuddered against her hand. "What a surprise. I believe she's free and easy with both."

"I turned her down. My price for picking her was that she let people think we'd slept together. That she'd seduced me. It seemed like an easy answer to get Lauchmann off your back and I don't really care who wins. And in a moment of bad timing you knocked on the door. I swear to you, before I turned my back to answer the door, her blouse was buttoned and her hair was combed."

Maggie *was* calculating and didn't hesitate to cause a scene. "But you had her lipstick on your mouth."

"I told you she offered me sex and I turned her down. I am not even remotely interested in Maggie Duchanne. In fact, the only woman I'm interested in is you. I meant it when I told you that every look, every touch in front of that camera was for you. Cutting that deal tonight with Maggie was for you. For us. If he thinks I'm sleeping with Maggie, then it doesn't matter whether he counts my condoms or checks my garbage. Maggie's just a red herring."

It made sense, but she also felt like one of those pathetic women who wanted to believe anything she was told as long as it exonerated her man. "It looked bad."

"I know. I'd just told her to convince everyone we were sleeping together. I could hardly tell her you didn't need to know. I'd told you I'd find a way to fix this and I did. I need to know you believe me."

Fine lines separated deep emotion. One seemed to mine another. Just as hate was closely akin to love, jealousy and anger shared space with passion. She'd known from the beginning that Rourke was temporary in her life, but it'd been a cold, rude awakening to see him with Maggie and think it was over. That she'd never know the feel of him against her, inside her: never again experience his touch, the taste of his skin, his mouth, his scent. And it galled her to know, even under those circumstances, that she wanted him as desperately as she ever had. "I want to believe you."

She still felt vulnerable, raw.

"How can I prove it to you?"

She needed to prove to herself that she was in charge of herself, of the situation. "You want me to trust you. But how much do you trust me?"

"I trust you implicitly."

IF HE HAD an ounce of pride, he'd tell her he didn't need to prove anything, especially since he hadn't done anything wrong. But, especially knowing her background, he knew trust wasn't an easy issue for her. "I'm at your command. Do with me what you will."

"Anything?"

"Within reason."

"Define unreasonable."

"Nothing immediately comes to mind. How about I'll let you know if we get there."

"Hmm." Something flickered across her face, a look of slight surprise, acknowledgment, sensuality. "What does this house remind you of?"

That was easy. They'd played it up often enough during taping. "A Moorish castle. Harems."

"Exactly. But do you want to know the really interesting part of the house?" she said, leading him to the bed. "It originally belonged to a woman who kept men for her pleasure." She practically purred the last word and it had the same effect on him as if she'd reached between them and stroked him.

He skimmed his hands over her shoulders, lightly touching her breasts. "Do you want me to be one of your men, brought in to pleasure you?"

"Yes." Her pupils dilated.

"I will pleasure you every way that I know how." He bent his head and captured a taut, pink nipple in his mouth and sucked. Her low moan floated over him and drove him to suckle harder. He did the same to her other breast until her breath came in hard pants. She pulled away and pushed him back onto the bed.

"You're willing to let me have my way with you?" Her eyes, more molten silver than green, seemed to shimmer.

He had a pretty good idea of who she was and what she was about, but he thought he'd better make sure she knew his boundaries. "I'm not into pain."

"Good. Neither am I."

She leaned forward, her hair a pale skein over his shoulders, her breasts teasing against his arm, her breath warm and fragrant against his ear. "I want to tie you to the bed with those cords holding back the curtains. Would you let me put you in bondage?"

She wanted to tie him up? He'd never tied or been tied. That meant he wouldn't be able to hold her, touch her at will.

"Please. Pretty please, with me on top." She flicked her tongue, warm and wet, against the rim of his ear and he was thoroughly seduced. At that moment he would probably agree to anything outside of cross-dressing or animals.

What did the actual restraints matter anyway? She'd already put him in bondage. A dozen women and all he could think of was her. This. "Yes. Put me in bondage."

She pushed him back onto the bed and he sank onto the sumptuous silk coverlet. She crawled onto the bed after him. Her hair hung over her shoulders, a silvery-blond curtain that teased him with glimpses of her breasts.

She used the silk cords that held the bed curtains in place and quickly bound his wrists and ankles to the four posts, leaving him spread-eagled and the two of them intimately ensconced, as the gossamer curtains shut out the rest of the room. And Portia was on to something because it was incredibly arousing to be simultaneously restrained and so open.

She tied the final knot and turned to face him. He felt as if thick, hot lava flowed through him. Her eyes were hot and glittery; she was as turned on as he was. "Are you comfortable?"

He tested his arms and legs. She'd left a generous amount of play in his silken bonds while still restricting his movements. "Just as cozy as a guy can be, spread-eagled on a bed with the woman he's desperate for just out of reach."

She crawled past his extended legs, her slender hip sliding along his erection with mind-blowing eroticism. She braced her hands on either side of his head and leaned down, veiling their faces in the fall of her hair. Her mouth descended on his in an openly sensual kiss. He unrestrainedly explored her mouth with his tongue, his lips, his teeth. She kissed him back with an abandon that maddened him. More than once he reached to cup her head in his hands, wrap her in his arms, pull her harder, tighter, closer to him. And each time he found his efforts thwarted by the cords binding him.

Longing filled his entire body. He ached for the feel of her satin nipples against his chest, something more substantial than the brush of her hip against his hard-on. He arced his body upward and for the briefest moment felt her body's softness and heat.

Portia pulled away from him. Rourke lost himself in sensation as she stroked his skin, laved him with her tongue, and kissed him all over until he was a writhing, heaving mass of nerve endings. It was the sweetest torture to see her moving over him, naked, but not be able to touch her, only to be touched by her.

The scent of their combined arousal was heady and filled the enclosed area. She leaned past the curtains and plucked a condom from the bedside drawer.

As desperately as he wanted her to sheath him, slide over him and enfold him in the hot, wet folds of her body, he wanted something else even more.

"Wait," he said. She paused, condom in hand. "I need to know that you believe me. If you can't trust me, don't take this any farther."

She wrapped one hand around his shaft and he clenched his teeth. "Yes. I believe you. I trust you." She slid the condom over him with the other hand and he wasn't sure which made him happier, that she trusted him or that they didn't have to stop.

9

FIVE LONG DAYS and even longer nights later, Portia finally was back in Rourke's bed, her leg wedged between his, still reeling from the residual tremors of her newfound experience of multiple orgasms.

"That almost made up for the wait," she murmured against the hard wall of his chest.

"Hmm. It's been five days of sheer hell," he said, his breath stirring against her temple.

He'd spent the last five days jetting from one exotic location to another on dates that lasted late into the night. Each night, Rourke and his date of the day had been in a posh hotel with connecting doors, giving him every opportunity for intimacy with that date. And, more importantly, precluding him from any real time alone with Portia. She'd missed the sex, and even more confounding, the times like this, the closeness afterward. She didn't want to think about next week, and the week after, and the months beyond. No, better to concentrate on the here and now.

"You're an odd man to call jetting to exotic locations with beautiful women, dining in five-star restaurants and staying in ritzy hotels sheer hell," she teased him.

He swatted her bottom playfully. "You know good and well it was because I couldn't be with you, but you need to hear me say it, don't you, you little egomaniac."

"I'd hardly qualify as an egomaniac, after watching all those women do their best to seduce you both on- and off-screen."

His expression grew serious. "I told you from the beginning, it's only you. I took your advice and became an actor playing a part." He threaded his fingers through her hair. "It's funny. When the studio offered me the show, it was simply two weeks that I had to get through. But now that it's almost over, I don't want it to end. And you know the part that I don't want to end? You. Meeting you on the terrace every morning. Waiting for you to knock on my door every night. The way the hair stands up on the back of my neck every time you walk into a room." He laughed. "The only worthwhile things that have happened have been on the terrace and in this room, because those were the two places that I've ever had you to myself."

Her heart knocked against her ribs. This was surely what was meant by making love with words. That was the most beautiful thing anyone had ever said to her other than her son's *I love you*. She swallowed past the lump suddenly blocking her throat. "I'll miss you as well."

"I have a day of down time after tomorrow's wrap-up. I'd like to spend that day with you." He laced his fingers through hers. "A day together without cameras and microphones where I can hold your hand when I want to."

No, no, no. This had been on-location fantasy. That felt too much like a date. And she didn't date. That hadn't changed. She still had her obligations. The rationale that had kept her on course for ten years hadn't changed. "I don't think that's a good idea. We're all under a gag order until after this program airs. And you're a celebrity these days. Paparazzi lurk in L.A. like vultures circling for a fresh kill."

"I know someplace where the paparazzi would never think to look."

She looked at him questioningly.

"Your place. Then I could hold your hand." He brought her hand to his mouth and kissed her fingers. It was gallant and tender and she felt herself waver beneath an onslaught of longing, both his and hers. "I could see where you live. Meet Danny. Maybe you could invite your parents and your sister over. I'd like to meet them all."

God, the sheer, absolute intimacy of letting him into her world scared her senseless. Why couldn't he just tell her he wanted one more day to simply have sex with her? That she could handle. Why wasn't it enough for him?

"I don't see the point. You're a nice guy and we've had a good time together, but I'm really busy and you live across the country and—"

"One day, Portia, please. Just one day out of a lifetime. What could it hurt?"

Me. If she wasn't careful it could hurt her. "I

don't know that it would hurt anything, but it complicates everything." She shook her head. "And you can't meet Danny. That's one reason I never dated. I didn't want to bring a procession of men into his life."

She saw the hurt in his eyes and hated that she'd put it there. She softened her tone and tried to make him understand. She didn't want to hurt Rourke, but she refused to hurt Danny. "I've seen it happen to so many kids. Their mom starts dating a man, the kid gets attached, the couple break up and the kid is devastated. Danny's already dealt with his father's abandonment. I have no intention of setting him up for further devastation."

He nodded. Solemn. Respecting her concerns and obligations. "Okay. So I can't meet Danny."

"How am I supposed to introduce you to my parents? They're understanding and fairly open-minded, but it could be awkward."

"Friends. You could try introducing me to them as your friend."

Except she didn't have any friends. Especially male friends. She worked and came home. "They're going to ask questions."

He drew a deep breath and she had a feeling she wasn't going to like what he was about to say. "Or you could introduce me as your lover. You're a big girl now, Portia. You're not seventeen and showing up pregnant. You're an adult woman who carries enormous responsibility and does a damn good job of it, but you are allowed a life and that includes a sex drive, honey."

She waffled. Part of her wanted to tell him her life was none of his damn business. Another part of her wanted to rise to the inherent challenge in his words. She didn't particularly want him at her apartment, but it was safer than a hotel, where he was much more likely to be spotted and identified. She was a nobody and the paparazzi didn't hang out at nobody apartment complexes. And it wasn't as if the apartment was really hers or was really personal. It was just a place until she and Danny bought their own home.

And once she ran through all of that rationale, she had to admit it was like standing at the edge of a deep, cold pool and testing the waters with your big toe. What would it be like to have him in her real world?

"I'll have to check everyone's schedule. I believe Danny has a Boy Scout camping trip planned." He missed her when she was gone but, nerd or not, he was a typical nine-year-old boy and after a hug or two was ready to get on with whatever he was into at the moment. And mom's return didn't begin to equal the allure of a scout camping trip. They were so on the brink of having a more normal home life when she got this studio position and didn't have location travel—their own place, a dog and no extended periods of being gone for weeks at a time.

"Thank you. I have this fantasy of spending the whole night with you. Of waking up with you next to me in the morning, your hair on my pillow."

Before Rourke, her full sexual experience had consisted of two times in the back seat of Mark's car.

Portia had never woken up next to a man. Never spent the night in a man's arms. Never shared her pillow when morning's first rays slanted through the bedroom blinds. Rourke's words painted such a picture that a frightening longing swept her.

She swept her hand to encompass his room. "Trust me, it's not the Taj Mahal."

He smiled. "It doesn't have to be, as long as you're there." His mouth descended on hers in a kiss so tender it stole her breath, and just possibly a little bit of her heart as well.

THE FOLLOWING MORNING, Portia had a hundred and one loose ends to tie up after they'd filmed the final episode where Rourke selected Maggie and then shot the final interviews. Terry and Jeff were busy disassembling wiring and the various sound components. Jacey and a helper had attacked the cameras. Climbing down from a ladder, Jacey handed the piece of equipment over to her assistant.

"Another reality wrap. Except for putting the show together next week," Jacey said.

"Yep. I'll be glad to sleep in my own bed instead of that brick that doubles for one. When are you heading back to New York?" She'd miss Jacey.

"I'll be here through the end of next week. I thought about flying back to New York for the weekend but Digg's on for twenty-four so I'm staying with the old man tomorrow. He spends every Saturday golfing. Want to do brunch tomorrow? You could bring your kid, if you wanted to."

Jacey had said once that she and Portia were a

good bit alike and it was true. They were both loners who tended to keep to themselves, but a friendship had developed between them on this set. During this shoot, Jacey had gone from being a coworker to a friend. Her abrupt brunch invitation delighted and surprised Portia.

"I can't. Danny's out of town and I...I have other plans." Portia, who kept her distance from everyone, went out on a limb. She reciprocated. "But maybe you could join me and Danny for dinner one night next week."

Jacey looked pleased at the invitation, but not too pleased because too pleased wouldn't be Jacey. "I guess I could do that. When is Rourke leaving?"

"I'm not really sure. You'll have to check with him on that."

"Oh. I was hoping he was your other plans."

Portia couldn't stop the smile that blossomed on her face. "He is."

Jacey grinned. "I knew it."

"He's so great, it's scary." Portia had spent so many years not confiding in anyone, now it was as if some dam had burst inside her and she was spilling her innermost thoughts with Jacey.

"I know exactly what you mean. Digg scared the hell out of me. Still does sometimes. If I was one of those sappy romantics, I might call Rourke your knight in shining armor."

Ha. If Jacey only knew about Nick, the real reason Rourke had appeared on the show. She had no idea. Rourke to the rescue? Was that how he saw her? The thought disquieted her. "I don't want a knight in shining armor. I don't need to be rescued." Being rescued implied a dependency on someone and she'd never put herself in that position. Particularly not with a man. That was foolish.

Jacey barked out a laugh. "News flash. Our men—" *Whoa*, Portia thought. *I wouldn't go so far as to call Rourke my man* "—need to save the day. It's in their genetic makeup. Digg's a firefighter, for God's sake. He donated most of the million bucks he won."

"You do know Rourke's an investment banker?"

"Digg's profession is overt. Rourke is a little more subtle, but it's there in that gallant courteousness that he extends to everyone. Why do you think women around the world are so apeshit over him? He's hot, but so are a lot of guys. It's because they sense that nine hundred years ago he'd be riding up on a white charger to take on the bad guy. That's what makes him really hot."

THE NEXT MORNING, Portia smoothed her hands over her shorts. She was a nervous wreck. A total basket case. He'd be here any minute. Bad decision on her part. She should've never agreed to let O'Malley come. This was different from the anonymity of being on location where she was in charge, where her position and wearing a suit every day allowed for retreat, regardless of whether she'd been naked the night before with Rourke.

Her doorbell rang. For a second she toyed with not answering the door, pretending not to be home. But not only was that a cowardly move, knowing

Rourke, he'd camp out on her doorstep and some-one was bound to recognize him sooner or later.

She opened the door. Backlit by the bright California sun, he filled her doorway. She'd seen him wearing a tux, faux sultan garb, bathing suits, khakis and button-downs, golf shirts, but she'd never seen him like this. This was the real Rourke and he looked better than he ever had. Worn jeans hugged his hips and a Boston Red Sox T-shirt that had seen its fair share of washings hung loose over his shoulders, the tail out.

The bottom dropped out of her stomach and she had no clue what to say. She felt positively naked without her suit and her clipboard.

He shifted from one foot to another and finally broke the silence stretching between them. "Hi."

"Hi." She needed either to invite him in or tell him to leave. She should really tell him she'd made a mistake and tell him to leave. That would show she still possessed some good sense. "Come in." She opened the door wider. His arm brushed her shoulder as he stepped into her apartment and her whole body tightened at the brief contact. "Did you have any trouble finding it? Traffic can be crazy."

He turned to face her and she leaned against the door she'd just closed. In the span of a single day she'd forgotten how very blue his eyes were, how thick were the black lashes that fringed them.

"No problem at all. My rental car has GPS and you forget, I live in Boston, where traffic is always hell. Getting to Logan airport around rush hour is a nightmare."

She nodded her head. "So, you're here."

He nodded back at her. "I'm here." His eyes flickered over her bare legs, her denim shorts, her cotton top with its scooped neckline, her hair in a ponytail.

He'd seen her naked any number of times, but with just that look, she felt more exposed than she'd ever been with him buried inside her. "Um, why don't I show you around? Trust me, that won't take long, and I can show you where to put your bag." She'd agreed to let him share her room, her bed. What *had* she been thinking?

"Sounds like a plan."

She swept her hand around the room. "This is obviously the den." And the furnishings were all obviously dated and secondhand and she felt slightly embarrassed. "I've always thought saving my money for a down payment was more important than new furniture, as you can tell."

Rourke laughed, somewhat self-consciously. "I'm an investment banker. The return is much better on real estate than on furniture. I own a condo with a view of Boston Harbor, but Watson's and my favorite chair is an old recliner we inherited when my dad got a new one from my mom to celebrate his retirement."

Some of the awkwardness between them dissipated.

He looked past her. She knew the series of framed black and whites on the wall behind the sofa had caught his attention. He walked over and bent one knee on the couch. For perhaps a full minute he knelt, immobile, studying the photos of her and Danny. Finally, Rourke turned to face her, the tenderness in his face nearly bowling her over. "They're beautiful. I can see you in him."

"He has my flat cheekbones and almond-shaped eyes, but for the most part he looks like Mark." He had Mark's dark hair and blue eyes and when he was concentrating very hard, which was often, he pursed his lips the same way Mark used to. "But he's very much his own person. My mother dabbles in amateur photography. She took a ton of shots that weekend and then mounted and framed those for my birthday. I love them."

"I can see why." He rose, but continued to stand in front of the sofa, looking at the photos. "How old was Danny?"

She smiled, thinking back to the day her mother had snapped the photos. "He was five. My parents treated us to a weekend in Morro Bay to celebrate my college graduation. It was one of the loveliest weekends of my life."

"You both look happy. It's obvious you're devoted to one another."

"I've met lots of single moms who think of their kids as mistakes. Mark was a mistake, but Danny never has been. He's a blessing. He's the most important thing in my life. I would die for him."

"Mark's a fool and Danny's a lucky kid." He glanced back at the photos and laughed. "I think I wore those exact same glasses when I was about his age. He reminds me a little bit of myself."

Portia knew, somewhere in her heart, without a

doubt, that Danny and Rourke would get along like a house afire. Rourke and Danny did share the same coloring and now that Rourke had mentioned it, they both had a way of intensely concentrating on one thing or one person at a time. The resemblance was enough that they could easily pass for father and son. And even thinking that way frightened her. She ignored his comment and walked through the open doorway into the tiny galley kitchen. "This is the kitchen."

He followed her, the space seeming all the smaller with his wide shoulders and scent surrounding her. He leaned against the counter and looked at the professional-quality stainless-steel cookware hanging from a rack. "Those are very nice. Do you like to cook?"

She was truly pathetic. The man was admiring her freaking *pots and pans* and she was getting all gooey inside.

"I love to cook. It relaxes me." She nodded toward the cookware. "A Christmas gift from my parents last year. They're wonderful to cook with. How about you?"

"It's a bit of a passion. I eat better than any single guy I know. That's one of the things I'm looking forward to when I get home. Some kitchen time." His smile held a shade of self-consciousness.

He was so cute when he looked that way, she couldn't help but tease him. "And do you clean up after yourself?"

"I live alone. If I don't do it, it doesn't get done." He was a nice geeky guy wrapped up in a gorgeous package and he liked to cook *and* he cleaned up after himself. It would be far too easy to fall in love with him and wind up with a shattered heart. She needed to keep it light and easy between them and she needed something to run with. "Do you have any vices?"

"Laundry. I hate to do laundry. I know it's the worst kind of waste of my money, but I send everything out," he said with a sheepish smile.

How could you hold that against a guy? "I don't know anyone who *likes* to do laundry."

Rourke shook his head. "That's because you've never met my mother. If she wasn't scared to drive in the city, I swear, she'd come in and pick mine up to do it."

"She sounds nice."

"She is. You'll like her." His eyes held hers.

Not *you would,* but *you will.* As if it was a given that she'd meet his mother. The thought sent her stomach into a nosedive. And just as she'd done before, she returned to her apartment tour without responding. A small hallway off the den and kitchen housed the bathroom and separated the two bedrooms.

"That's Danny's room," she indicated the closed door but didn't offer to let him look inside. That was Danny's private space and she had no right to share it with someone without his permission. "Obviously the bathroom." She led him into her room, her private sanctuary, her haven. "And this is my room." She realized he was still carrying an overnight bag. "You can put your bag over there," she said, pointing to a spot beside the closet.

He dropped his overnight bag and looked around her room. His assessing gaze seemed to take in everything, from the cool greens and blues of the framed sea abstracts on the wall to her platform bed with its simple coverlet in a soothing aquamarine. "Your place suits you. Elegant but not fussy."

His words pleased her. "Thank you."

The air, the energy between them changed. They were in a bedroom, familiar ground for them.

"Portia, why do you always wear your hair up or pulled back?"

"It stays neat and contained that way." She glanced around the room. "I'm a bit of a neat and organizational freak in case you haven't noticed."

"I did. But I knew that already. You couldn't do the job you do without those traits."

She smiled, inordinately pleased by his observation. "And I bet your place is a bit of a mess."

He grinned. "Guilty. How'd you know?"

"Your toiletries were scattered in your bathroom on the set."

"I'll try not to be a messy guest." He started toward her and her heart began to race. "Can I do something?"

"What's that?" He hadn't even reached her and she was already breathless.

He cupped her shoulders in his hands and she sighed inside at the heat of his touch. Without thought, she caught one of his wrists in her hand and brushed her cheek against his knuckles and pressed a kiss to the springy dark hairs on his wrist.

He half moaned and half sighed. "Oh, Portia...I want to take your hair down."

Rapunzel, Rapunzel, would you let down your hair so that I can scale your fortress walls and wreak havoc in your well-ordered universe until I and the pleasure you find with me, in me, through me become your universe?

"Rourke, I'd like you to let down my hair."

HOLDING HER GAZE, he worked the elastic band out of her hair. He buried his hands in the mass as it tumbled past her shoulders. "I love your hair. It's beautiful."

He didn't give her a chance to respond. Instead, he did what he'd wanted to do since he'd walked through her door—he kissed her. Her mouth was as sweet, her kiss as potent as he remembered. Maybe more so. His tongue swept the recesses of her mouth, rediscovering her taste, exploring her. She sucked on his tongue and he felt the sensation in his groin. Oh, God, one kiss and he was hard.

He pulled away from her, his breath uneven. Neither said a word, but instead they began to undress. Rourke made quick work of his jeans. He stepped out of his shoes and pulled off his briefs and his socks. Once in a moment of passion, he'd forgotten his socks. Mary, his college lover, had scathingly told him that dress socks on a naked man were not sexy. He'd never forgotten again. He sent a silent thank you to Mary because Portia was looking at him as if she found him quite sexy at the moment.

She'd taken off her clothes and was lying on the bed on her side, propped on one arm, blatantly admiring him. "You could pose for a sculptor."

He was damn glad she felt that way, even though it wasn't a remote possibility. "I don't think so."

"But you're beautifully proportioned." Her hot gaze lingered on his recently lengthened portion and he felt damn near light-headed as all the blood in his body seemed to rush to pool between his legs.

"I could be convinced if you were the one doing the sculpting," he said.

She wet her lips with the tip of her tongue and shifted to her back, canting her legs, her glistening sex beckoning him. "Rourke."

He bit back a groan. When she spread her legs that way he could barely think, barely breathe, it made him so hot. He could feel the heavy beat of his heart, feel the ache that started somewhere inside him and manifested itself in his throbbing member. The musky scent of arousal hung in the air. He stood still, immobilized by the sheer beauty of her. "You are perfect."

She opened her mouth and he could've sworn she planned to argue with him over his statement. Instead she murmured, "Thank you."

Rourke looked down at her, letting everything he felt show. It was important to him that she know how he saw her. "You're like an exotic goddess who's deigned to reveal herself to a mere mortal."

Okay, maybe he'd spent a little too much time immersed in Arthurian legend and Tolkien before he'd discovered sci-fi. Thank God she didn't laugh at him. Instead there was a glimmer of tears in her eyes. Shit. He'd rather she laughed at him than know he made her cry. Good job, dork boy, take her from lusty to weepy in six seconds or less.

He knelt on the coverlet beside her and spoke without measuring his words. "Oh, baby, please don't cry. I never meant to make you cry."

She blinked away the moisture and smoothed her hand over his jaw. "Rourke, don't make me out to be something I'm not. I'm just a flesh-and-blood woman. I'm not a goddess. And I'm far from perfect, inside or out."

She was perfect—for him. "The way I see it, you *look* perfect." He skimmed his hand down her shoulder, over one rounded breast, down her belly, past the slightly darker blond curls between her thighs, and the length of her leg. "I don't know. You *feel* perfect."

He nuzzled her neck and she dropped her head back with a soft sigh. "You *smell* perfect."

Slowly, deliberately he lowered his head to one perfect breast with its perfectly tempting nipple and licked her. "Hmm. *Tastes* perfect." He went back for seconds and was gratified by the shudder that swept her and her low moan of appreciation. He raised his head, a teasing note beneath the heat that threatened to consume him. "Ah. I hate to tell you, but you *sound* perfect as well."

"Okay, okay. I give up. I'm the perfect embodiment of womanhood," she said, a sexy glint replacing the tears that had been in her beautiful eyes earlier.

"Hmm. I'm so glad you decided to see things my way." He smoothed his thumb over the fullness of her lips, moving up to the exotic flat planes of her cheekbones.

She slid her leg beneath his, her thigh nudging his heavy erection. She reached beneath her pillow and pulled out a wrapped condom. "You're very convincing." She opened it and smoothed it over his hard sex. He quivered against her hand. "Like water dropping on a stone."

He pulled her other leg over his hip, opening her thighs to him as they faced one another. "Water dripping on a stone. That's not very flattering."

She inched her leg higher, opening herself wider. "You wear me down."

She had no idea. In one smooth thrust, he was buried inside her. "I'd much rather wear you out."

10

OH, SHE DIDN'T KNOW when she'd ever felt this good, except maybe every time she was in bed with Rourke.

"I'm ravenous," she said, stretching and rolling out of bed. "I'm going to cook an early dinner. Do you want to help?" She pulled on her shorts and T-shirt but left her hair down and bra and panties off.

"I thought you'd never ask."

He looked like a kid who'd just been handed a Christmas present and her heart flip-flopped.

"You were waiting for me to ask? Since when have you not just gone after what you wanted?"

He grabbed her wrist and pulled her down on top of him, his hands molding to the small of her back. "How hungry are you?"

Laughing she twisted away, "Very. And if you plan to help you'd better get up and put on some clothes."

He raised his arms and pillowed his head on his hands. "No naked chefs?"

He was too sexy for her piece of mind. Even the thatch of dark hair in his underarms sent a shiver through her. She shook her head, her gaze traveling across his broad chest, down his rippled abs, further still to his lean hips that showcased his sex, impressive even when flaccid, surrounded by dark hair, those muscular thighs that tensed to rock-hard every time he came…. Maybe if all she had to do was pop a frozen dinner into the microwave it'd be okay, but serious cooking, where she needed to actually have a clue? No way. "No naked chefs. I'd definitely be too distracted."

Looking extremely arrogant and extremely satisfied with her answer, he stood and pulled on his jeans and T-shirt. He blinked. "Damn. I just lost a contact."

Both of them dropped to their hands and knees and cautiously felt around on the carpet, searching for the lost lens without success. After a few minutes Portia sat back on her heels. "Do you have another pair with you?"

"No. I have a pair of backup glasses but they're…"

"They're what?"

"I look like Rourke the Dork in them."

"Can you see without them?"

He grimaced. "You resemble a Monet painting on a really fuzzy day."

"For God's sake put the glasses on."

"But I'm telling you—"

"Put…the…glasses…on."

"Okay. I'll put on the glasses." He grabbed a contact lens case and an eyeglass case and disappeared into the bathroom. In a minute he was back, wearing a pair of black-rimmed glasses.

Portia took a deep breath. She hadn't been kidding about having a thing for geeks. She'd only thought O'Malley was good-looking before. He was devastating now. "You look like Clark Kent."

He turned a delicious shade of red. "I told you—"

She backed him up to the wall outside the bathroom door and pressed against him. "You don't understand. I have a serious thing for Clark." She pressed a hot, hard kiss to his mouth.

He looked kind of stunned and very sexy when they both came up for air. "I may never take these glasses off."

"As long as you keep them on—" she ran her hand down his body and stroked him through the denim "—later."

He appeared faintly dazed. "Oh, honey, you just say the word and I'll wear them 24/7."

Laughing, feeling young and sexy and carefree, Portia led him to her kitchen. "I thought I'd make a sage- and rosemary-stuffed pork loin, roasted potatoes and fresh asparagus. I went to the market this morning so I'm well stocked. Any preferences, suggestions?"

"What if I provide dessert?"

He was mouthwatering in those glasses and jeans and T-shirt. She glanced at him suggestively. "I was counting on you for dessert."

He grabbed her and pulled her against him, kissing her. "You are a wicked woman."

She kissed him back. "Only since I've met you."

He slid his hands beneath her shorts and cupped her bare buttocks. "Do you have any heavy cream?"

He slid one hand between her thighs, his finger testing the wetness that was beginning to gather there.

Her breath hitched in her throat. "Yes. I keep it on hand."

"Ideally it should chill overnight but I could make a crème brûlée."

She gripped his shoulders as he stroked one finger against her. "I like crème brûlée."

His gaze flickered from the bowl of fruit at her elbow to her nipples stabbing against the thin cotton of her shirt. "Or your pears look nice and ripe. I could make a pear tart." He bent his head and dragged his tongue across her nipple, leaving a wet mark on her shirt. "Why don't you think about it while I put on some music?"

She should have protested, but she'd never prepared a meal in a semiaroused state before. She knew exactly what was for dessert and it was very erotic.

"There's a CD player in the armoire in the den." Her voice was husky, the denim between her thighs wet. "My sister works for an electronics retailer so she gets great deals on equipment. The hip-hop is Danny's and I'd rather skip that. The rest is mine, so anything you pick out is fine."

While Rourke plundered through her CD collection, Portia pulled herself together, decanted a bottle of wine and gathered the ingredients for their meal.

"This is one of my favorites," he said from the other room. She didn't ask, just waited to hear what came on. She immediately recognized the opening chords to a Dave Matthews Band selection.

Rourke stepped back into the kitchen and she smiled her approval. "I love this CD. How about a glass of merlot? I noticed during the filming that you seemed to prefer that." She preferred the richness of reds to whites as well.

"You noticed what wine I prefer and you have it?"

"Yes." Wow. Amazing how a small detail could please him so much. And amazing how it made her feel like an accomplished geisha. She poured each of them a glass and for a while they enjoyed wine, music, aimless conversation and cooking together, and always the potent sexual chemistry simmering between them as they brushed arms while working at the counter, his hip skimming against her buttock as he leaned over the sink.

The song "Crash into Me" came on and Rourke wrapped his arms around her from behind, linking his hands beneath her breasts. "This is how I feel. Like you crashed into me before I knew what happened." His warm breath stirred against her ear, sending a hot shiver down her spine. "That's exactly how I feel around you. Tied up and twisted." Relaxed from her wine, she cupped her hands over his, leaned her head back into the crook of his shoulder and gave herself over to the lyrics, the man, swaying in time to the music.

The song ended and Portia realized she was still wrapped in his arms, her eyes closed. There was something so romantic, so tender, so far beyond mere sex in leaning into him, swaying to the music, that she didn't know how to react. She released his hands and disentangled herself, getting back to business in the kitchen.

"You said you wanted to meet my parents and they're dropping by this afternoon."

Without her asking, Rourke washed the potatoes in the sink. "I'm looking forward to meeting them. Do they live nearby?"

She handed him a cutting board and knife. "Close but not too close, if you know what I mean." She began to mince the herbs. The pungent scents of rosemary and sage filled the kitchen. "I picked an apartment that was in the same school district as their house. Since Danny stays with them when I'm on location, I needed to make getting him to school as easy as possible for everyone. They're dropping off a science project he'd started that's due next week."

"Do they know I'm here?"

"I didn't get that far." Portia stuffed the roast and Rourke stepped over to lend a hand with the kitchen twine. "When you meet my mother you'll understand. She talks fast and she talks a lot." And Portia'd been a chicken. She didn't want to have to explain Rourke. And what if he hadn't shown up? Then she'd have mentioned him when it was totally unnecessary. She washed and dried her hands. "And anyway, I'm an adult. Having a…friend over isn't a big deal." She leaned down and put the roast into the oven. Rourke slid the dish of potatoes in beside it.

Rourke looked almost stricken. "Do you date often? Is there someone special?"

She'd deliberately misled him when they'd first shown up on location. They were far beyond that point, and he deserved better. He deserved the truth. "No. I don't date." She cleaned up the counter and bagged the leftover herbs. "I'm busy and Danny's my priority and men can't handle that. And I refuse to parade a retinue of men through Danny's life. It's not fair to him." She reiterated what she'd told Rourke once before. "He's already had to deal with a dad that doesn't want him. I won't have him dragged into the disappointments of relationships that don't work out for me." That should give Rourke a pretty clear view of what their outlook was and reassure him she wasn't going to chase him across the country.

He propped against the kitchen counter, his arms crossed. "But doesn't that mean you might never find the one relationship that does work for you?"

She shrugged. "My lifestyle works for me now. Very nicely. Just like your lifestyle with Watson works for you."

Behind the glasses, his eyes narrowed and she could literally see the wheels turning. Good Lord, he was impossibly attractive in those glasses with his hair messed, wearing a T-shirt, worn jeans, and bare feet.

"If you don't date, what about sex?"

Portia felt a blush wash her neck and color her face. What was he thinking, asking questions like that? "I don't have any sexually transmitted diseases and outside of that, it's none of your business."

"You know I wasn't asking about STDs." She could see him putting two and two together and coming up with exactly four. "When was the last time you made love before us?"

She turned her back to him, without answering. He slid his arms around her from behind, enveloping her in his body heat, his scent. "Has there been anyone since Danny's father?" he asked. "There hasn't been, has there?"

The hard ridge of his arousal pressed against her buttocks. He was actually getting turned on at the idea of her not having sex in forever. He brushed his hands across her belly, feathered them over her ribs to cup her breasts. He bent his head, his breath warm against her neck. "Why me, Portia?"

Trapped between the counter and his big, hard body, with his hands on her breasts and his mouth against her neck, she could barely think beyond the feel of him against her.

He nibbled at the nape of her neck and rolled her nipples between his fingers and she grew even wetter and hotter. She didn't have enough…whatever…left to make up a lie. Sexual turn-on as a truth serum. "Because you're across the country. Because it was my last location assignment. And because I wanted you like I've never wanted any man before." The last word ended on an incoherent moan as he ravished her neck.

"Was Mark the only one before me?" He suckled the nerve-rich nape of her neck while his fingers continued to torment her through her shirt. She gripped the edge of the worn countertop.

"Yes." She pushed against him. God, he made her feel so good, so alive, so unlike anything she'd ever experienced before. And it was tacky and crass, but Mark deserved no less, and neither did Rourke. "Mark was the only one. Twice. And it wasn't very good."

"Oh…" he groaned against her neck, unzipped her shorts and slid them down her hips, leaving her naked from the waist down. He turned her around. His face was hard and flushed with arousal. "I may have signed up to bring the dessert, but I know what I'd like for an appetizer."

His big hands spanned her waist and he lifted her to the edge of the sink. Surprised, she instinctively braced herself, grabbing the lip of the counter, her heart thundering. He knelt between her thighs, hooking one knee over each of his broad shoulders, exposing her to him. He parted her with his thumbs and looked up at her, a carnal smile on his face, his blue eyes hot and glittery behind those sexy, black horn-rims.

"Something sweet." His warm breath gusted against her and she grew wetter still. "Something ripe and juicy." His thumbs traced her folds. *Please. Please.* "Nectar." He blew gently on her and she almost bucked off the edge. "You." He swiped his tongue along the path of his fingers, the faint scrape of his beard against her inner thighs intensifying the pleasure. She dropped her head back, her "Yes" echoing off the ceiling.

Rourke was a handy man to have in the kitchen.

THE FOLLOWING MORNING, he woke slowly, instantly knowing where he was and who he was with, but wanting to savor the sensation of his first time waking up next to Portia. Because this would be only the first time of many, despite the fact that she'd picked him because he lived over two thousand miles away.

He concentrated on the heat of her naked body pressed against him, the length of her smooth, feminine leg between his, the silk of her hair against his shoulder and chest, her scent that wrapped around him, the fine cotton of the rumpled sheet beneath him, the soft down of the comforter thrown over both of them.

Careful not to disturb her, he reached one arm to the nightstand and groped for his glasses. When he put them on, he found her watching him. "Sorry, I didn't mean to wake you," he said. "I can't see without them and I wanted to look at you. You're just as beautiful as I thought you'd be." He shook his head. "No. That's not true. You're even more beautiful."

A sweet blush washed over her. He could bring her to a rousing, screaming orgasm time and again, but a simple compliment seemed to embarrass her.

"You might need to check that prescription on those glasses when you get home," she said, self-consciously raking her fingers through her hair.

He smoothed a few stray strands from her shoulder as much to prove to himself that this was real and not some dream. He was here in Portia's bed. "Have you been awake long?"

"A while. I'm not used to sleeping with anyone. And you're big." He grinned when she glanced at the sheet tented by his early-morning hard-on. "You take up a lot of room."

"Good thing you're just the right size." He propped himself on his elbow and looked down at her. Drinking in the sight of her. "I think your parents liked me."

They'd dropped by just before dinner the previous evening. Jack and Laela Tomlinson were nice folks who obviously doted on Portia, Danny and Portia's sister Mellina. Portia had inherited her mother's looks and her father's fair hair and reserved demeanor. Although they'd been cordial and gracious, more than once he'd caught the older Tomlinsons exchanging glances. His poor baby was in for the third degree when he left.

She nodded nonchalantly, but he noted the wariness in her eyes. "Everyone likes you. You're that kind of guy."

"I think it's a bonus that they liked me, but I really only care whether *you* like me." He tried to tease the wariness away.

She scraped her fingernail lightly over his belly. "One would assume that I like you well enough, considering you're naked in my bed."

"Umm. Hold that thought," he said jumping up and heading for the bathroom. If this were one of those romance novels his mother liked to read, he wouldn't have to hop out of bed to relieve himself. But it wasn't and he did, so he made quick work of it. He caught a glimpse of himself in the bathroom mirror. Damn, he looked rough. He needed to shave and his hair was standing up on his head at odd angles. The glasses gave him a mad-scientist look. Make that a naked mad-scientist look. But he was hoping to talk her into for better or for worse and she was definitely getting a glimpse of the worse. He shrugged and hurried back before Portia decided to get up and get dressed.

Luckily for him, she was still nestled under the covers. He slid in beside her, pulling her into his arms. "Now where were we?"

She smiled, her hand curling over his hip. "If my memory serves me correctly, we were talking about you being naked in my bed."

He laughed but inside he felt as nervous as a thirteen-year-old geek with a crush on the pretty girl. If he had a piece of paper, he'd write her a note asking her if she'd go steady with him and give her the yes and no boxes to check her answer. Instead he simply asked her, "Do you like me enough that I'll wind up here again?"

She shifted away from him and propped her back against her pillow. "I do like you, but that's really not a good idea."

"I think it's an excellent idea."

She looked away from him, her fingers absently plucking at the edge of the sheet. "Rourke, let's not complicate this. We've had a good time—" he uttered a protest and she looked at him "—okay, a great time together, but I have obligations and you have obligations and let's just leave it at a good time. Anyway, the show won't air for several weeks and there's that gag order."

Okay. He was going for broke. Laying his cards

on the table. "Couldn't we at least talk on the phone? Perhaps see each other every couple of weeks?" He laughed, amazed that now that the time was upon him, he was surprisingly calm. "See, I've got this problem. I love you." Portia's eyes widened and her mouth gaped slightly. "I think I'm one of those love-at-first-sight poor sots because I haven't been the same since I saw you and I'm damn sure I'm not ever going to be the same again."

She slowly shook her head *no*. "Rourke…"

He bulldogged ahead. "And I'm pretty sure you love me, even though I'm even surer you don't want to admit it."

Her chin rose, and he glimpsed a shadow of that cool haughtiness she'd armored herself in from the beginning. "Why would you assume I love you just because we had great sex together?"

Aha. She did consider it great sex. "Because you couldn't make love to me the way you did if you didn't love me. Some women could, lots of women do and there's nothing wrong with that or with them. But that's not the way you're made, Portia." He'd known last night in the kitchen when she'd admitted that there hadn't been another man since Mark. From her comments over dinner, he knew she thought he'd had some caveman response to her having only one man before him, but it was the knowledge that he had to mean something to her that had excited him so. "Otherwise you wouldn't have waited this long to let a man back into your bed, because, honey, we both know you're neither repressed nor frigid."

He wasn't sure if it was the "repressed or frigid" bit, but it was cute when this elegant woman's mouth gaped like that. He cupped her cheek in his palm. "We could have a good life together. Me, you and Danny. I'm not wealthy, but I do okay. We'd be comfortable enough. And maybe one day we could give Danny a little brother or sister, or both."

She held up both hands and shook her head. "Wait. Whoa. Stop. Are you talking about mar… You mean you'd want to… Let me get this straight…"

He almost laughed at her stumbling around the concept of marriage as though it was something she couldn't give voice to. "Marriage. Married. Wedlock. Matrimony. Yeah, that."

"You don't even know me."

"Yes, I do. And you know me. I know the things about you that matter. I know you're a woman of integrity. A hard worker. Independent. Intelligent. Passionate. A great mom. We both come from similar backgrounds. We both believe strongly in family. We're both very good in the kitchen."

She flushed but patently ignored his kitchen comment. "I don't have any interest in marriage," she said, gazing at the seascapes rather than him.

She didn't have to look at him. As long as he could keep her talking and she didn't just clam up, all wasn't lost. "Why?"

She looked at him then, and he willed himself not to flinch at the starkness of her eyes. "It wouldn't be fair to you. There's a certain amount of trust and vulnerability required for a marriage to work and I can't…I won't go there."

"Let me—"

She cut him off. "I'm not some damsel in distress, Rourke. I don't need rescuing. I don't need to let you do anything."

She damn well didn't need to stay locked up in this fortress she'd built for herself, holding everyone at bay. But he had enough sense to keep that to himself. "I don't want to rescue you. I just want to love you."

"I'm not so sure that those aren't one and the same for you." Okay, so she was a very smart woman. "Jacey says you have a white-knight complex. You have to rescue people and I think she's right." Rather than be offended, he was heartened that she had talked to Jacey about him. She scrunched her knees up beneath the sheet and wrapped her arms around them, becoming a self-contained unit. "Can't you see that I don't *need* to be rescued? I don't *want* to be rescued? I learned the hard way that I can count on my family and I can count on me. It wasn't an easy lesson and I don't plan ever to repeat it."

She'd laughingly referred to him as water dripping on a stone, then so be it. "We'll take it slow. All I'm asking for is a chance to prove that you can trust me, that I'll still love you as much next week as I do now. Probably more."

"I like to think of myself as a person of integrity. How can I take and not give in return? What kind of person does that make me? And you'll get tired of giving with nothing in return."

He reached out and smoothed his hand over the

line of her bare back. She was warm satin beneath his fingertips and he felt her quiver at his touch. "That's the thing. It's not a choice. It's a part of me. One of those involuntary functions like the hypothalamus functioning on its own, breathing, my stomach digesting my food and moving it on to the intestines." He caught himself. He'd definitely slipped into total geek mode, but her eyes had softened and she'd loosened her death grip on her knees. "I'm just Rourke the Dork in love with the pretty, brainy girl who sits in the front of the class and doesn't give him the time of day. You're the one with the Vulcan mind meld."

She reached out a tentative hand, her fingers curling around his, her hand small and delicate compared to his large, dark one. "I don't want Danny brought into this. I don't want him hurt if this doesn't work out."

His heart slammed against his ribs. He reminded himself to breathe. Okay, so maybe it wasn't an entirely involuntary function. "Fair enough. This can work, Portia. I just need you to tell me that you'll give us a chance."

She brought his hand, still clasped in hers, to her lips. She pressed a gossamer kiss to his fingers. "Okay. I'll give us a chance."

It wasn't a yes, but it wasn't an unequivocal no either. They were the sweetest words he'd ever heard.

11

PORTIA RETURNED the vacuum cleaner to the hall closet, her apartment tidy, organized, everything back in its place. Rourke had left for Boston an hour ago and she had another hour and a half before she had to pick Danny up from his camp-out. She pulled the elastic out of her hair—what the heck, she was beginning to like it hanging loose around her shoulders.

She missed Rourke, missed knowing that she wouldn't see him tonight, or tomorrow morning, or even the day after that. She turned on the CD player, skipping ahead to track seven, "Crash into Me." She was practical, pragmatic, logical. She didn't do silly stuff like moon around, but she couldn't seem to stop herself, and, quite honestly, she didn't want to.

She flopped on the sofa and wallowed in missing him. She closed her eyes and inhaled his scent still clinging to her skin, her clothes, remembering the timbre of his voice when he declared that frightening *I love you*. The blue of his eyes when he'd pulled her to him as he left, as if he couldn't bear to leave, couldn't bear to let her go.

And now he was gone and she felt as bereft as if a dark cloud had rolled in and denied her the sun's warmth. And the damnable part of it was she didn't know when there'd be another sunny day in her forecast.

The phone rang. She answered the portable on the end table without getting up.

"Hi," Rourke's voice slid over her, through her, around her.

She was glad she was alone because she was absolutely helpless to stop the smile that felt a mile wide. "Hi. What are you doing calling me?"

"They're boarding my plane, but I wanted to hear your voice one more time." His voice dropped. "What are you doing?"

"Lying on the couch."

"Are you dressed?"

Laughter burbled up from her at his strained tone. "Yes, I'm dressed." She stepped out on the ledge. "But I'm thinking of you."

His indrawn breath echoed over the line. "I hope it's good."

She inched forward, closer to the scary edge of the precipice. "I miss you."

"Oh, baby. I miss you too." She heard a speaker announcement in the background on his end, the words indecipherable. "Listen, I've got to go or I'm going to miss my plane. I love you, Portia."

"I…uh…I miss you. Have a safe flight."

Another loudspeaker announcement. "Bye."

"Bye."

She clicked the phone off and lay there, floating on a cloud. Things like this didn't happen to her.

The phone rang again in her hands, startling her.

She answered it, laughing. "Get on that plane, you insane man."

A short pause on the other end. "Portia?"

Uh-oh. Maybe she'd sign up for caller ID regardless of the expense. "Hi, Mom."

"I take it Rourke has left?" her mother asked with wry amusement.

She'd noticed her mother mentally taking note yesterday when Rourke had mentioned his flight time. Portia braced herself for her mother's inevitable one hundred and one questions. Actually, she wasn't up for this now. "I'm not feeling quite up to speed. Could I call you later?"

"Well, then lie down while you talk to me."

Humph. She should've known her mom wasn't letting her off the hook that easily. "I'm trying to be a good mother and give you some space, but when I see my daughter looking happier than I've seen her in years, I think I deserve to know something about the young man that put that sparkle in her eyes."

Whatever this was between her and Rourke, wherever it was going, it felt too fragile, too new for her to pull out to be examined under her mother's microscope.

"Mom, it's just like I told you and Dad when I introduced you, he just finished two weeks on-site and was having a little decompression time before he headed back to Boston. In Massachusetts. Where he lives. End of story."

"Portia Renata Tomlinson, I am your mother but I'm not a simpleton. Rourke looked at you like you hung the moon. Looks don't particularly impress me, never have, never will. But I recognize a man with a good heart when I see one, and it was easy enough to see that in him. Your father and I discussed it and we'll be happy to have him as a son-in-law."

What? Portia's mouth hung open. She closed it with a snap. "Son-in-law?" What was up with everyone talking marriage today? "You'd marry me and Danny off to the first man who seems interested in me?"

"No. Don't be silly." That was more like it. "But we'd willingly marry you off to the man you're in love with."

Surely she'd heard that wrong. "Excuse me?"

"I said we'd marry you off to the man you're in love with."

"I'm not… That isn't… You're wrong." Portia liked him. Obviously. There was a lot to like about him. But love? Love?

"I'm your mother. I think I know my own daughter."

Portia sputtered. Sometimes her mom was nuts. "I'm me. I think I know me."

Her mother harrumphed her disagreement. "Sometimes it's hardest for us to know ourselves."

"Let's say for one wild moment that you were right. Rourke lives in Boston. You would send me and Danny to Boston? You're all the family my son has. You would tell me to rip him away from all that he knows, all that he holds dear, to live with a stranger?"

"I would tell you that I would rather have a

happy daughter in Boston than a daughter only half alive in LA. And I would tell you that it's time for you and your son to build your own family, for your son to see his mother happy, for your son to have a father and know that being a father is more than donating sperm."

That threw her for a loop. "But you met him for half an hour—"

"And it was plenty of time for me to see the most important thing." Her mother's voice thickened, as if clogged by tears. "Mark snatched my bright sparkling daughter from us ten years ago and now your Rourke's given her back."

"SHE'S THE ultimate woman. Beautiful, smart, sexy," Rourke said.

Nick smirked, shaking his head. "Man, you've got it bad."

Rourke grinned. "Yeah, I do." Watson wiggled down beside him a little more in the chair.

"And you're giving up your contacts cause she likes the geek glasses?"

Rourke remembered the way Portia had backed him up against the wall, the press of her lithe body against his, the hungry heat of her kiss. Most definitely he was converting to glasses. "Yep."

"Man, you're going to spend a small fortune flying out there." Sprawled on the leather couch, Nick put his feet on the coffee table, nudging aside an empty pizza box. Rourke was messy. Nick was a slob.

"No, I'm not." He couldn't stop grinning. He gave the chair up to Watson and walked over to the

floor-to-ceiling windows that spanned half of the
wall and showcased the spectacular night view of
Boston Harbor. That view alone had enticed him to
buy the condo that had once been a factory. He
turned his back on it to face Nick. "I'm going to
spend a small fortune moving out there."

Nick sat up straighter and rubbed the back of his
neck. "You're serious aren't you?"

"Never more serious in my life."

"But what about mom and dad? Boston's your
home. Your family's here." Nick crossed his hands
over his belly. "Hell, I'm here and I'm your baby
brother."

He nodded. "Yeah, but she's there."

"But you said she's got a kid and the dad's a
deadbeat and doesn't support either one of them at
all. Do you know how much money having a kid,
especially one who's not even your own, is going
to cost you?" Nick asked.

For the first time, Rourke questioned the wisdom
of having bailed his brother out of his predicament.
Nick just didn't seem to get the big picture. "When
you love someone, you don't look at them as an investment. When you love someone you give them a
check for half a million dollars because you love
them."

Nick had the grace to look ashamed. "Okay. So
when do we meet this paragon you're forsaking us
all for?"

"I don't know yet." He could envision months
before he could talk her into it and even then it'd
probably be kicking and screaming.

"You're not like one of these stalker guys who's gone off the deep end are you?"

Nick should've definitely been the one to appear on the show, with his penchant for melodrama.

"One day you'll fall in love and know what it's like to love someone body and soul. To look at them and know you're seeing your destiny."

"I'm happy for you. Truly I am. And you've always been the one to take care of everyone. God knows, you saved me when I was up to my ass in alligators, so I'm telling you now, this woman better treat you right or she'll answer to me."

Maybe there was hope for Nick discovering he wasn't the center of the universe. "You're just sulking. Trust me, you'll love her."

"How can you be so sure?" Nick quirked a dark brow.

"Because I do."

"Monday mornings suck and this one sucks even more than usual. We've got a big-ass flop on our hands, boys and girls."

A hard knot formed in Portia's gut at Lauchmann's grim expression. He was a jerk, but he was a jerk with an unerring nose for turning out winning TV programs.

"I spent the weekend reviewing the footage. Forget any promotions—" Lauchmann eyed her directly "—or any pay raises. If we don't pull a miracle out of our asses on this one we'll all be lucky to get a job filming termite mounds in the bloody Sahara. Hell, Mueller's going to have all of our heads." Portia looked across at Jacey, who raised her eyebrows and gave a small shrug. "The studio spent a small fortune on this."

"What's the problem? The filming seemed to be going well." Portia asked the question everyone wanted to, but was afraid to insert into the midst of Lauchmann's tirade.

"The freaking problem, as I freaking see it, is that we freaking lost him. He was hot. You could feel the sexuality rolling off him on the camera. He was really hot, and he was seducing the women of the world. And then he bagged Maggie and that on-screen sizzle was gone."

Except O'Malley hadn't "bagged" Maggie. It'd been Portia. She'd screwed herself out of her promotion, perhaps even her job. Literally.

"What would it take to fix it? What'll it take to save it?" she asked when she could breathe again.

"A damned miracle would be nice. We need to make chicken salad out of chicken shit."

He really was a sorry excuse for a human being. "Could you be a little more definitive?" she asked. What the heck? If she was about to lose her job or any chance of imminent advancement, why not go out with a little backbone? And this was the creep who'd wanted her to hide in the bushes.

Lauchmann shot her a nasty glance. "The first few episodes will rock. We need something to stir the pot for the last half. Some juicy gossip. Some dirt. We'd better come up with something or we can all start packing for Africa."

Portia felt like a sleepwalker waking up. This

was the real world. Not some fantasy spun by a blue-eyed, dark-haired man. Promises from O'Malley wouldn't pay her rent, keep food on her table, or clothes on her and Danny's backs. That was her responsibility. It always had been, it always would be. She'd be a fool to watch her job go down the toilet while she clutched some postorgasmic promise from O'Malley. Let the sex cool and he'd reconsider anyway.

"Everyone get the hell out and I don't want to see any of you until you've got a solution to this total screw-up." Lauchmann dismissed them with a sharp wave of his hand.

She depended on herself. She'd screwed this up for herself, now she'd fix it.

Portia kept her seat while everyone filed out posthaste.

Lauchmann glared at her. "What do you want?"

Portia got up and closed his door. "I want to save our collective ass." There was no reason she should feel a kinship with Judas. O'Malley would do the same, wouldn't he? This was business.

Lauchmann sat forward, eyes gleaming. Odd how they reminded her of thirty pieces of silver. "Spill."

This was her job, her livelihood. She opened her mouth. This was her integrity, her self-respect. She could find another job, but if she lost her integrity…and hell no, O'Malley wouldn't do the same. She might not have it in her to be what Rourke wanted her to be, but she certainly didn't have it in her to destroy him and his family. "I thought we could brainstorm."

"I thought we could brainstorm," he mocked her, throwing her a look of total disgust. "Get the hell out and don't come back until you've got something for me."

If she really wanted an exercise in integrity she'd tell Lauchmann to take his show and his job and shove it. But her heroism only stretched so far. She had bills to pay. She got up and left without another word.

Jacey straightened up from where she was slouching against the wall outside Lauchmann's door. She fell into step next to Portia. "What was that about?"

"That was about the dumbest thing I've ever done. How do you feel about filming termite mounds in Africa?"

Jacey shrugged. "I'm not crazy about hot weather and I don't like bugs." She cast a sidelong glance at Portia. "So what was that really about?"

Portia knew Jacey could take the information straight to the top, to Burt Mueller. And it really wasn't her secret to confide. But she needed to talk to somebody, and she considered Jacey a friend. She trusted her.

She led Jacey into her office and pulled the door closed behind her. "I could've saved the show, our jobs. Would you like to thank me now or later for letting you sink with the rest of us?"

Jacey dropped into a guest chair. "I guess I'd rather hear the whole story before I thank you up front."

Portia told her about Nick's embezzlement, what it meant to Rourke's family and the role Rourke played in it. Jacey smirked. "I told you he was a white-knight kind of guy."

Like a classic horror-movie scene, her office door swung open and Lauchmann entered, clapping his hands. "We're back in the game. Good job, P.T. We've got a scandal and a white knight charging in to save the day. Apparently I should've taken you up on your brainstorming offer, 'cause that's a helluva solution." Lauchmann rubbed his hands together, reminding her of a giant insect. Cockroach.

Bile rose in her throat. "That's private information."

"Don't disappoint me. We both know that's good PR. Excellent work." He tossed her clipboard onto her desk. "You left that in my office. Good thing I had to take a piss and was nice enough to stop by with this."

He started out the door and turned around to face her. "You know, I'd have to fire you if I thought you weren't going to share your news with me." There was nothing nice about his smile. "But I'm going to assume you would've told me sooner or later because I really don't want to fire you. Good help is hard to find. In fact, I believe you just earned your promotion." With another unpleasant smile, he left them.

"What a dick!" Jacey said.

Portia couldn't manage more than a nod. Lauchmann was a dick. They had a hit. She had her promotion. She jumped up and ran for the bathroom.

She only made it as far as her trash can before she threw up her breakfast.

ROURKE FINALLY gave up after reading the same page for the third time. He put the book on the coffee table and leaned back to listen to his copy of the CD they'd listened to at Portia's place. His head wasn't in a book, it was with her.

Work had been a zoo today. Mondays were always hectic and he'd hustled his butt to play catch-up after two-and-a-half weeks away. Even with his demanding schedule, she'd never been far from his mind. He'd toyed with calling her several times since he'd been home. But damn it, thanks to Nick's comment, he didn't want her to feel like he was some crazy psychopath stalker. On the other hand, he knew as surely as he knew his own name that while she'd promised him a chance yesterday, doubts and fears would begin to crowd her today. And without him to allay those fears, they'd gain the upper hand, and he'd slip back down the slope he'd worked so hard to gain ground on.

He glanced at the clock. Fifteen minutes past midnight. Only a little past nine on the Pacific coast. To hell with Nick, he was calling. He picked up the phone and dialed her number. Cripes. His heart was pounding.

"Hello," she answered the phone, her voice a balm that soothed his soul.

"Hi. It's Rourke."

"Rourke…what are you doing up so late?" She sounded tired. Strained. Agitated.

"Missing you. Were you busy? Is this a bad time?"

"No. No, it's fine. Danny's in bed and I was just folding some laundry."

"Ah, my favorite. Did you miss me today?"

"Yes. I mean, I don't know. I was really busy today. Listen, I was going to call you tomorrow—"

"That's good news—"

"Listen, don't say anything else." He heard her draw a deep breath and knew he wasn't going to like what he heard. "I have something to tell you."

"Okay. I'm listening. But you're not going to tell me anything that's going to change my mind." She really had no faith in his feelings.

"There's a problem." Foreboding knotted his gut. "We had a meeting at work today. Lauchmann spent the weekend reviewing the show. The bottom line was that the second half was a bomb, the part filmed after you and I slept together. Lauchmann told us all our jobs were on the line, that we needed something to save it from being a bomb."

A chill ran over him. He knew what was coming before the words left her mouth. "Let me guess. Lauchmann knows about Nick."

"Yes. He knows." Her voice was barely a whisper.

"How could you, Portia?" Pain, sharp and real, sliced through him and he lashed out. "I trusted you. You of all people should know what it feels like to have a trust betrayed."

"I didn't tell him, Rourke. He overheard me—"

"But if you hadn't been talking he couldn't have heard could he, Portia? I told you that in confidence."

"If I could take it back I would," her voice sounded cool, distant formal, "a thousand times over. But do you want to know the best part of this? I had the opportunity to tell him. I was going to tell him, Rourke. I closed the door and sat in his office and when it came down to it, I couldn't. Not to save my job, not to save the show."

He laughed, bitter, disillusioned. "You know, if you had just called me up and talked to me instead of talking to someone else… I would've probably told Lauchmann myself if it would've meant saving your job."

"So, what's this really about, Rourke? Is it about me betraying you or me taking away an opportunity for you to save the day?"

"Damn it, Portia. It's about trust. I trusted you. Trust—you know, the concept that's foreign to you? Do you still have your job? Did my news get you your promotion?"

"Yes. I have my job and I got the promotion. I told you before I don't need you to come to my rescue."

Her tone, positively glacial, fed his ire. "That's all that matters, isn't it? That you can continue to barricade yourself in your own insular world." He laughed, almost choking on his own rancor. "I thought you were beautiful and brave and a woman of integrity." He closed his eyes, disgusted with himself. He'd failed his parents and his brother. "I was wrong, and now my family will pay the price for my foolishness. I want you to think of what you've done to my parents every night before you go to sleep."

"Are you through?" Was that a hint of tears behind her cool tone?

He thought of his mother standing in line at the grocery store she'd shopped at for years, her family's disgrace screaming at her from every tabloid lining the check-out line, the whispers and the stares that would follow and he hardened his heart to Portia's tears. "I'm almost through, but not quite. You surround yourself with shields. At work you hide behind that damn clipboard. And you hide behind your son. You know, you're so afraid of letting anyone come into contact with Danny. You're afraid to show him to me. Honey, what should really frighten you is what you're turning into."

12

PORTIA HUNG UP the phone. Moving like a zombie, she stripped naked and climbed in the shower. Only then did she give way to the tears she'd choked back. At first she cried silently and then great gulping sobs shook her. She curled into a ball of misery on the tiled floor, welcoming the sting of spray on her back. She sat on the shower floor until there were no more tears and the water ran cold.

Rousing herself, she climbed out and dried off. She wrapped the towel around her, leaving her hair dripping past her shoulders. She leaned against the sink and swiped a spot on the steamed mirror. The reflection was watery and murky, but she stared at the woman. Did she know her? Did she like her?

Rourke's words had left her raw and bleeding because in great measure he was right. She *had* cut herself off from everyone. And she wasn't proud of this particular truth, but she *had* hidden behind Danny.

What kind of role model was she setting for her son? Should she show him by example that the only way to go through life was at a distance? Safe, but alone? Was that what she wanted for him when he

was a grown man? Alone? An island to himself?
Did she want him to view need as a strength or as
a weakness? She had only seen it as weakness, but
with Rourke it felt like a source of strength. Today,
she'd almost made a decision she wouldn't have
been able to live with. She'd almost told Lauchmann, willingly, knowingly, to his face. Did she
want to stay in a position where that kind of betrayal was valued? Where the reward for wrecking
someone's life was a promotion? If she stayed, how
long before that corporate culture nibbled away at
her integrity until she became another Lauchmann,
digging through garbage, real and figurative, to get
ahead? She would, thank you very much, prefer
filming African termite mounds.

And then she faced the truth that even in this
moment of reckoning she'd put off. She loved him.
She loved Rourke O'Malley. Beyond reason. Beyond redemption. Whether she wanted to or not.
He'd been angry and hurt, but she also knew how
much his family meant to him, and exactly how
humiliating Lauchmann's revelation would be to
those people he loved.

The old Portia would have retreated behind her
wall. The old Portia would have been almost grate-
ful that it had come to this, happy for an excuse to
amputate the feelings he roused in her, to seek an
out and take it.

But she wasn't that same woman. Maybe that
was part of the involuntary thing Rourke had tried
to explain. No matter what their outcome, she was
a different woman. His love had marked her,

changed her. She wasn't the same and she couldn't go back to the life she'd had for the last ten years. Nor did she want to.

We could have a good life together. Me, you and Danny. And maybe one day we could give Danny a little brother or sister, or both.

She embraced his sweet words and the pictures they conjured. She allowed the fantasy she'd clamped down on to play out in her head. Her and her two geeky guys, Danny and Rourke. And baby makes four? What would it be like to have her belly swollen with a child whose father wanted it? A pregnancy filled with joy and anticipation, rather than fear of the unknown? How would it feel to know she would share all the trials and tribulations of parenthood rather than face them alone?

She had told Rourke she didn't need him to rescue her and she didn't. But it was high time she rescued herself.

Rapunzel had let down her hair and now that she had a taste of what lay beyond the fortress walls, she didn't want to go back.

"So, IT'S DONE. And it can't be undone." Rourke sat on the edge of the sofa upholstered in a cabbage-rose print in what his mother called the front room, his hands loosely linked between his knees.

He looked from his mother to his father and was stunned at the amused glance that passed between the two of them. "I think I haven't done a very good job of explaining this. Obviously I haven't, because there's nothing funny about this situation. When you go to the store, Ma, it's going to be on the front page of every tabloid. Your neighbors will never look at you the same."

His father gave him a censoring look. "Your ma and I fully understand how serious this is. I can't say that we're very proud that Nicky would do such a thing. We know we raised him better than that, but we're not about to die of shame, the way you think we are. No. Your ma and I think it's funny that you lads thought we didn't know and how you thought you had to protect us from knowing."

Rourke was damn glad he was sitting down. "You knew? When? How?"

"Probably about the same time Nicky confided in you. A man called the house one day," his mother said.

"But if you knew, why didn't you say something?"

"It was up to Nick to bring it up to us. And when a man makes mistakes, he has to learn to handle them on his own."

"But we're family. We take care of our own."

"When you and Nick were little we took care of you when you scraped your knees. Then you got to the point when you took care of your own scrapes. A family sticks together, but ultimately a man has to account to himself for the decisions he does and doesn't make. At the end of the day, he has to be at peace with who he is and what he does. Your ma and I can't do that for you or Nick. You can't do that for your brother."

Rourke nodded. He was finally figuring out that

he hadn't particularly done Nick a favor. "I'm beginning to see that."

"There's always been a bit of an inequity in your senses of responsibility. You always had too much and Nick never had enough. Rourke, you've always wanted to rescue things since you were a wee lad. But sometimes rescuing people undermines them. Makes them think they can't do it themselves. Sometimes sinking on his own does a man more good than swimming with help."

He glanced from his mother to his father. "Well, this is going to hit and it'll be up to Nick whether he sinks or swims."

"I believe your brother is made of sterner stuff than you think." His father shot him a loving but censuring look. "Just as your ma and I are tougher than you seem to think."

"And now enough about us and Nick. Tell us about this lass of yours," his mother said.

And he found himself telling them about Portia. Her background, Danny, her parents, everything. Everything except the sex. They were, after all, his parents. "I said something that I shouldn't have. I was angry and hurt. I don't know if she'll forgive me. I was harsh."

His mother smiled at him, soothing him with her calm. "Well, if you love her, and it sounds like that's the case, all you can do is ask."

He was ashamed of the way he'd lashed out at Portia. He gave voice to his greatest fear. "But what if she won't forgive me?"

"Then you ask some more," his mother said.

His dad nodded. "Grovel if you have to. And you keep asking. Trust me son, pride makes for a cold bedfellow."

PORTIA SAT in the coffee shop across from Rourke's apartment building. She hoped he got home soon before she totally lost her nerve. She hadn't called him. What she needed to say had to be said in person. But nothing she'd done today had made her as nervous as facing him. Of course, while important, none of the rest of the day mattered as much as he did. A light rain began to fall, darkening the sidewalk, clinging to the leaves of the tree outside.

A garden of umbrellas blossomed, making it harder to see the faces of the passersby. What if she missed him? Just as the thought occurred to her, she felt him, soul-deep, an instant before she saw him walking down the sidewalk. Her heart did a slow somersault in her chest—or at least it felt that way. She was excited and nervous and she wondered if a heart could actually beat out of a chest.

Was he still angry? Was he too hurt, too betrayed to even give her a chance? What if he refused to let her in? The old Portia whispered that she could just walk in the opposite direction, catch a cab and arrive at Boston's Logan airport early for her flight back. Safe. Familiar. Alone. The new Portia, however, straightened her spine and marched across the street.

ROURKE TOSSED his jacket and his shirt and tie across the closed toilet seat and pulled a clean towel off the hook to dry his hair. His mother had insisted he be home before six tonight. Something about her having a package delivered to his house and it couldn't be left at the door. He would've been more curious, possibly paid more attention, if he hadn't been so stinking miserable over Portia. He desperately needed to apologize, but it wasn't something he wanted to handle over the phone. He needed to be face-to-face with her. He couldn't afford a weekday off work, and he could ill-afford the weekend with all the catch-up he had, but Saturday would find him on her doorstep, groveling, trying to salvage something of their relationship from the mess he'd made.

The door buzzed and Watson started barking madly. Towel in hand, Rourke went to the front door. Before he even looked through the peep hole, the hair on the back of his neck stood up. He looked through the hole and for a second thought he was hallucinating.

"Portia?" He threw the lock and opened the door. "Portia? It really is you?"

A thousand butterflies took flight in his belly and he was literally dumbstruck.

Watson sniffed her rain-spattered pumps. "Watson, I presume."

Rourke nodded as the dog lost interest and trotted back into the den.

She took another deep breath, shifting the package in her hand. "Can I come in?"

"Oh. Of course. I'm stunned… I wasn't expecting…"

She stepped past him and he closed the door, turning to face her. She lifted her chin and without preamble said, "I love you."

He had behaved like such an ass. She was so cautious. Surely his head was playing tricks with him. "Say that again."

Her eyes a dark gray, serious, she repeated herself. "I love you."

Galvanized into action, desperate to make it real, he dropped his towel, crushed her to him, and kissed her as if his very life depended on it. Or perhaps that was the way she kissed him. He lifted his head. "Say it one more time."

She smiled. "I love you."

"Oh, God, Portia. I love you so much. I'm so sorry I said the things I did. I was going to show up on your doorstep on Saturday and beg your forgiveness. I thought it was too important for a phone call."

She nodded. Would they always be on this same wavelength? He thought so. "That's why I'm here."

"I'm so sorry. I was—"

"Right. You were right. They needed to be said. I thought I was meeting life head-on but I was simply existing in my tower."

For the first time since she'd shown up on his doorstep, he really looked at her. She looked the same—beautiful—yet, different. A softness had replaced the wariness that had always lurked in her eyes. Her hair fell in a rain-damped curtain past her shoulders. "Your hair is down."

She nodded, almost shy. "I've adopted a new style."

"I like it. It suits you." He slid his hand along her cheek, loving the brush of her hair against the back of his fingers. "You are impossibly beautiful."

"Thank you." She drew a deep breath. "I've got a couple of things to tell you and two things to give you. And I'm really not sure how you'll feel about any of them." She knotted her hands together, uncertainty replacing her former radiance. "You may want to sit."

"Okay." He realized they were still in the foyer and he was shirtless, but she'd seen him in less. Getting dressed wasn't nearly as important as what she had to say. "I'm sorry. Let's go in here." He led her past the kitchen to the den. Neither, however, sat. Watson regarded them from the recliner with dark-eyed interest.

She wet her lips with the tip of her tongue. "First, I need to tell you that I went to see your parents today."

Stupefied, he sat. "You went to see my parents? Here? Today? Why?"

"I wanted to apologize for what was coming down the pike and the role I played in it."

His heart swelled with love, pride and gratitude for her courage, for what it must have cost her. "Oh, honey, they don't blame you. And neither do I." He shook his head at how he'd missed the big picture before, but seeing it very clearly now. "Nick created this mess and I made it worse."

"That's about what they said. They're nice people. Once I got past being so nervous I thought I'd throw up, I enjoyed my visit with them." She smiled, a spark of devilment lighting her eyes to more green than gray. "Your mother showed me pictures."

Rourke felt a dull flush crawl up his face. "Please tell me she didn't show you my graduation picture." He had been at his all-time geekiest. Skinny with braces and glasses. And a bad haircut to boot.

Portia smiled and nodded. "Baby pictures to present day. You were cute."

She had seen those pictures and she'd still told him she loved him? "Ma could've left me with a little dignity."

"She's proud of you."

Eager to shift her attention from those photographs and curious as to what other surprise she was about to throw his way, he prompted her, "You said you had something else to tell me."

"Yeah." Another one of those deep breaths. "I'm about to be unemployed."

What the hell? She was damn good—no, great—at what she did. "Those bastards *fired* you?"

"No. I'm quitting. I'm pretty sure I can find another job. In fact, I dropped by for an impromptu visit at the local PBS station here."

This was better than he'd ever dreamed. But it all felt surreal, as if he couldn't trust any of it. "Here? In Boston? Five blocks from here?"

"It seemed about like that. I got a little disoriented with the cab ride." She reached into the bag she'd carried since she'd walked in and pulled out her clipboard and held it out to him. "I want you to have this. I don't need it an more. But it makes a very effective shield if you're in the market for something like that."

He took the clipboard he'd accused her of hiding behind.

She pulled out something else, a book of sorts. "And I'd like to introduce you to my son. This is a picture album I've kept since Danny was a baby. I thought maybe you could meet him here and then come out for a visit...get to know him...maybe we could all go to a ballgame or...well, something."

Suddenly elation and peace both flooded him. He'd been scared to trust any of this, even her declaration of love, but at this moment, when she offered not just herself, but her son, the person she held most closely, most dear, to him, he knew she was as sure as he was.

"Oh, honey..." He dropped to one knee and took her hand between his. "Portia fair, will you rescue this poor besotted white knight? Will you and Danny save me from being a crusty old bachelor who spends his Friday nights switching between *X-Files* and *Star Trek* reruns?"

Her smile illuminated his world. "You have women chasing you and tossing their underwear at you. You just had your choice of the world's wealthiest, most beautiful women, but you want me to save you from yourself." She shook her head, as if he amazed her. "Well, maybe we can cut a deal. I'm in desperate need myself of a white knight. Not to rescue me, mind you, but to cover my backside."

Epilogue

"DAD, WHICH WAY would be better to set up the lab table?" Danny asked.

Portia looked up at her two favorite men in the whole world setting up Danny's new lab center in the corner, next to the bank of windows that showcased Boston and its fascinating skyline. Just as she'd anticipated, it had been total adoration from first sight for Rourke and Danny.

Rourke caught her eye and beamed. One of the sweetest moments of her life had been when her son had shyly asked, on their wedding day, if he could now call Rourke Dad. And her strong handsome hunk of a husband, labeled by women around the world as "really hot," had cried. In the three months they'd been married, Danny couldn't seem to say it enough and neither she nor Rourke ever tired of hearing it.

She put down her new clipboard, a gift from her husband. Her production notes for the week's shoot could wait until later. She got up from her spot on the couch where she'd been sandwiched between Watson and Shirley, Danny's mini-schnauzer Rourke had helped him pick out at the rescue center, and wandered over to her two guys. "How's it going?"

Rourke looked up, his eyes shining. "Great. Boy genius here will be blowing up the place in no time."

Danny punched his stepfather in the arm, obviously pleased by Rourke's affectionate teasing. "Mom, look at this." Danny showed her a piece of equipment, which was a total mystery to her.

"Pretty cool, huh?" Rourke asked with enthusiasm.

She had no idea about the equipment, but Rourke and Danny geeking out together thrilled her. "Very cool. This has been some birthday, huh?" She wrapped her arm around her son's thin shoulders.

He hugged her back before pulling away. "Awesome. I'm glad grandma and grandpa were here. I think they liked our place. And I could tell, they liked Ma and Da too."

Rourke's parents had insisted from the beginning that Portia and Danny call them by the names their sons did—they were, after all, family now.

"Yeah, they seemed to get along well together," she said.

"That's an understatement," Rourke said. "My parents are having a blast. They're even talking about buying a motor home so they can travel with Laela and Jack. I never knew they were interested in that kind of thing at all."

Portia laughed, shaking her head. "You? Mom and Dad had never mentioned wanting an RV. Of course they wouldn't have." No, it had taken her getting on with her life and developing her own family to free her parents up to pursue their dreams. Jack and Laela Tomlinson had made the trip from L.A. to Boston to celebrate Danny's birthday in their new motorhome. Moira and Paul had invited them to park it in their yard in Quincey, since Boston's narrow streets didn't exactly accommodate RVs. "I'm glad they like one another."

"Surprised?" Rourke asked.

"Not really."

Danny joined in without looking up from where he was lining up empty beakers. "It's perfect. Grandma talks all the time and Grandpa's kind of quiet. Da likes to talk but Ma doesn't say much. It all works out." He glanced up with a satisfied smile.

Rourke slipped his arm around Portia's waist. "That's one smart kid."

Danny looked up and smirked, obviously pleased at Rourke's comment. She'd once thought of herself as a sponge soaking up Rourke. They were a family of sponges now.

Rourke nuzzled her temple and a familiar tingle shot through her.

"Yuck. You guys are gonna start that kissing business."

Portia laughed. They didn't have make-out sessions in front of Danny, but she and Rourke were openly affectionate. Her son needed to see how people in love, who respected one another, interacted. She kissed Rourke's jaw. "I think we just might."

"Double yuck. Can I go up to Jason's and finish this later? His mom invited me to come over after my grandparents left. I told her I had two sets and she congratulated me."

Jason lived one floor up, and though he was a year younger than Danny, the two boys were kindred spirits. "If she invited you…"

Danny was off and running for the front door. "She did," he called over his shoulder. Two seconds later the door banged closed behind him.

Portia laughed and threw her arms around Rourke's neck, all the happiness inside her bubbling over. "This is the best birthday my son's ever had."

"It *was* good, wasn't it? I think he likes Ma and Da."

Portia snorted, blowing a strand of hair out of her face. "What's not to like? They spoil him shamelessly."

Rourke grinned and lifted her in a bear hug. "Honey, I'm so happy. I told you we'd have a good life together."

"Hmm." She ran her hands beneath his shirt, plying her fingers along the muscles rippling below his skin. A familiar delicious heat stole through her. "That was sweet of Jacey and Digg to take the train up from New York for the party. She's gotten to be one of Danny's favorite people."

Rourke skimmed his hands along her back and her breath hitched in her throat. "Do you think she'll marry Digg before the baby comes?" he asked.

Portia laughed. "Probably. But you know Jacey. It'll be on her terms."

Rourke cupped her fanny and pulled her into intimate contact with his lower body. Moisture gathered between her thighs. He nuzzled her neck. "Remember that little brother or sister we'd talked about for Danny?" he asked.

"Yeah. In a couple of years. Why?" She wanted another child. His. But she also wanted them to have their time first. "You know how I am about schedules."

He slid his hands around her waist and eased down her zipper. Her heart thundered against the broad wall of his chest. His unerring fingers slipped inside her. "If you could work it into your schedule, I thought we could get in a little practice."

She had that dizzying sensation of her entire body tightening and beginning to unravel at the same time. "I could definitely work it in. I've heard practice makes perfect."

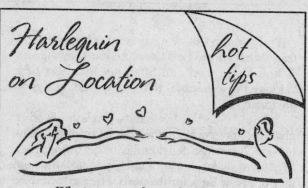

Harlequin on Location

hot tips

Wherever your dream date location,
pick a setting and a time that won't be
interrupted by your daily responsibilities.
This is a special time together. Here are
a few hopelessly romantic settings to
inspire you—they might as well be ripped
right out of a Harlequin romance novel!

Bad weather can be so good.

Take a walk together after a fresh snowfall or when it's just stopped
raining. Pick a snowball (or a puddle) fight, and see how long it takes
to get each other soaked to the bone. Then enjoy drying off in front of
a fire, or perhaps surrounded by lots and lots of candles with yummy
hot chocolate to warm things up.

Candlelight dinner for two…in the bedroom.

Romantic music and candles will instantly transform the place you
sleep into a cozy little love nest, perfect for nibbling. Why not lay
down a blanket and open a picnic basket at the foot of your bed? Or
set a beautiful table with your finest dishes and glowing candles to set
the mood. Either way, a little bubbly and lots of light finger foods will
make this a meal to remember.

A Wild and Crazy Weeknight.

Do something unpredictable…on a weeknight straight from work.
Go to an art opening, a farm-team baseball game, the local playhouse,
a book signing by an author or a jazz club—anything but the humdrum
blockbuster movie. There's something very romantic about being
a little wild and crazy—or at least out of the ordinary—that will
bring out the flirt in both of you. And you won't be able to resist
thinking about each other in anticipation of your hot date…or telling
everyone the day after.

Are you a chocolate lover?

Try WALDORF CHOCOLATE FONDUE—
a true chocolate decadence

While many couples choose to dine out on Valentine's Day, one of the most romantic things you can do for your sweetheart is to prepare an elegant meal—right in the comfort of your own home.

Harlequin asked John Doherty, executive chef at the Waldorf-Astoria Hotel in New York City, for his recipe for seduction—the famous Waldorf Chocolate Fondue....

WALDORF CHOCOLATE FONDUE
Serves 6-8

2 cups water
½ cup corn syrup
1 cup sugar
8 oz dark bitter chocolate, chopped
1 pound cake (can be purchased in supermarket)
2–3 cups assorted berries
2 cups pineapple
½ cup peanut brittle

Bring water, corn syrup and sugar to a boil in a medium-size pot. Turn off the heat and add the chopped chocolate. Strain and pour into fondue pot. Cut cake and fruit into cubes and 1-inch pieces. Place fondue pot in the center of a serving plate, arrange cake, fruit and peanut brittle around pot. Serve with forks.

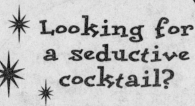

Looking for a seductive cocktail?

hot tips

Try *Ero-Desiac*—
a dazzling martini

With its warm apricot walls yet cool atmosphere, Verlaine is quickly becoming one of New York's hottest nightspots. Verlaine created a light, subtle yet seductive martini for Harlequin: the Ero-Desiac. Sake warms the heart and soul, while jasmine and passion fruit ignite the senses....

The Ero-Desiac

Combine vodka, sake, passion fruit puree and jasmine tea. Mix and shake. Strain into a martini glass, then rest pomegranate syrup on the edge of the martini glass and drizzle the syrup down the inside of the glass.

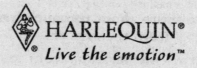

An Invitation for Love

hot tips

Find a special way to invite your guy into your Harlequin Moment. Letting him know you're looking for a little romance will help put his mind on the same page as yours. In fact, if you do it right, he won't be able to stop thinking about you until he sees you again!

Send him a long-stemmed rose tied to an invitation that leaves a lot up to the imagination.

♥

Autograph a favorite photo of you and tape it on the appointed day in his day planner. Block out the hours he'll be spending with you.

♥

Send him a local map and put an *X* on the place you want him to meet you. Write: "I'm lost without you. Come find me. Tonight at 8." Use magazine cutouts and photographs to paste images of romance and the two of you all over the map.

♥

Send him something personal that he'll recognize as yours to his office. Write: "If found, please return. Owner offers reward to anyone returning item by 7:30 on Saturday night." Don't sign the card.

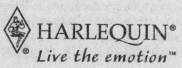